650

domestic tr
value of $2

4151 8282

MW00721488

1. Read Steve Bedwell's contributions to this collection and answer the following question:
What did Cheryl take to the party?
(tick one box)

☐ her neighbour's pink and grey galah
☐ a yellow, ribbed condom
☐ a lovely sponge
☐ her fire engine red Monaro

2. Name your favourite story in
Great Australian Bites

_____

Name _____

Address _____

_____

Post your entry to: Great Australian Bites Competition, PO Box 320, South Fremantle WA 6162.

Entries close last mail received 31 July 1997. The winning entry will be drawn in Fremantle on 1 August 1997. The winner will be notified by mail and their name published in the *Weekend Australian*, 9 August 1997.

GREAT AUSTRALIAN BITES

EDITED BY
DAVE WARNER

FREMANTLE ARTS CENTRE PRESS

First published 1997 by
FREMANTLE ARTS CENTRE PRESS
193 South Terrace (PO Box 320), South Fremantle
Western Australia 6162.

Consulting editor Clive Newman.
Designed by John Douglass.

Typeset by Fremantle Arts Centre Press
and printed by Prime Packaging Industries Pty Ltd.

National Library of Australia
Cataloguing-in-publication data

Great Australian bites.

ISBN 1 86368 191 4.

1. Australian wit and humour. I. Warner, Dave, 1953- .

828.3020803294

The State of Western Australia has made an investment in this project through
the Department for the Arts.

CONTENTS

ACKNOWLEDGEMENTS

Many thanks to Linda Martin for her assistance in the development and coordination of this project through its preliminary stages.

'Benchmark' is an adaptation of a piece that Rob Sitch first wrote for *Business Review Weekly*. Santo Cilauro's 'Wrestling' is an adaptation of a piece that first appeared in the *Sunday Age*. 'Tragedy' is an adaptation of a piece Clinton Walker first wrote for *The Edge*. 'Congress' by Dennis Altman first appeared in *Island*. 'Turn the Other Cheek' by Shane Maloney first appeared in *Arena*. 'Science is a Health Hazard' was written and performed by Lex Marinos in an ABC TV debate. 'The Rebirth of Australian Cricket' is an extract from the Coodabeen Champions' radio show. 'Riding Rooting King' by HG Nelson first appeared in *The Sporting Doctor*.

INTRODUCTION

Once upon a time I was in Beppu. Beppu is not a Mongolian word meaning 'deep shit'. Nor is it mythological, like say, Camelot. There is no trick to Beppu. It is a small resort town in Japan, famous for its hot, therapeutic springs and favoured by elderly country bumpkins for their holidays. A sort of Blackpool of the Rising Sun.

My travelling companion's daughter was dancing with an English troupe as part of a Vegas-style variety show which played twice every day at one of Beppu's prominent tourist hotels. Despite the glittery leotards, the plumed headgear, the dripping marcasite and the Bluebell legs, the dance troupe was received like a headmaster on speech-night, dutifully yet without enthusiasm. Mind you, the audience didn't like the musicians much either. Nor the singers — unless they were crooning some traditional number, which to the unenlightened Aussie had the feel of 'Harvest Moon' in three keys simultaneously. There were a couple of stand-ups too whose routine was, of course, in Japanese. They didn't like them either. What the audience did find uproariously funny was the comic acrobatic routine. Especially where it appeared the male acrobats had fallen on their goolies and were in deep pain. The more the feigned pain, the bigger the laugh. Every fall, every show, every day.

I didn't find this funny, just vaguely disturbing. What I found funny was the sight of the hotel guests piling into taxis in their hotel kimonos and getting driven to the town centre so they could cram into karaoke bars and sing their lungs out, never to ridicule but always to polite applause from fellow guests in their kimonos.

Years later, travelling on a flight from Sydney to Perth, I saw middle-aged men in business suits with tears of laughter streaming down their faces as they watched *Mrs Doubtfire*, the in-flight video. In case somebody on this planet hasn't seen the movie, I should explain that it is a story where Robin Williams is in drag, acting as his kids' matronly housekeeper. In a scene where Mrs Doubtfire's fake breasts catch aflame, entire rows of businessmen went into convulsions. I guess I found the scene mildly amusing, but certainly not as screamingly hilarious as my fellow passengers. What I thought *was* screamingly hilarious was all these Armani-suited men, in hysterics, choking on those inedible Anzac bikkies the airlines pass off as food.

What am I saying here? I guess maybe only

this: regarding humour, elderly Japanese agrarians and fifty-year-old frequent-flying Australian businessmen may have more in common with one another than with me.

Japanese farmers and flying businessmen aside, we are optimistic that in *Great Australian Bites* you will find much to delight. Contributions range from the mischievous, to the scandalous, to the ludicrous.

If you can bear with me, and consider humour as a cricket match, then this book should give you a fine day's play for your bucks.

From Steve Bedwell's glorious little poetic late-cuts for two, to HG Nelson's massive hyperbolic tonk over the sightscreen, from Linda Jaivin's beautifully flighted wrong'un on amorous revenge, to Santo Cilauro's corker-yorker on TV Wrestling, it's all there.

In the outer, his face painted green-and-gold, Tim Smith is singing this country's simple pleasures, Mark 'Jacko' Jackson is at the bar regaling the crowd with improbable tales of a yob's rise to Hollywood stardom and Jacqui Lang is eavesdropping in the sponsors' tent for dirt for her gossip column. Barry Cohen is trying to avoid the cameras in case his missus catches a glimpse of him on the screen, while Greg Macainsh is definitely tampering with something in his pocket. Paul Dempsey is selling defective sun-visors, Rob

Sitch is keeping score, Max Cullen is phoning through his story, Damien O'Doherty is dodging missiles, Bruce Beresford is reliving the torture of childhood cricket-induced sunburn, and Hugh Lunn is poking about in the dressing- rooms where Roy Slaven is belting players with a heavy bat, in a motivational speech that makes Hitler look like Alexander Downer.

There will almost certainly be passages of play not to your liking. Craving the brute bash of the one-day game, you may be the sort to fast-forward past the defensive prod and the delicate glances that characterise some pieces. Conversely you might thrive on such understatement and cry foul at the crude imposition of genitalia — as some literary streaker crosses your line of vision.

But whatever your particular preference, as the dark clouds of the impending last-page gather and the umpires check their light meters, I'm hopeful you'll still be yelling 'play on.'

DAVE WARNER

Tim Smith

AUSTRALIA, A TERRIBLE PLACE TO VISIT BUT I WOULDN'T MIND LIVING THERE

Last year I was offered a job overseas; it took me a minute to think it over, before I graciously declined. But what a full minute it was, 'cause in that sixty seconds I realised that I truly, madly, deeply, love this joint.

So here we go, a sixty second thought process roughly translated to paper ...

'So, do you want to stay here and work with us?'

Hmmm. Shoot through. Nick off. Bundy. Ark it. Vamoose. Follow the wide open dollar. Wear the 'Expat hat'. Leave Australia. Hard.

No one else in the world's like an Australian, not even those insidious bailers, the expats, because let's face it, how much money is it worth to:

Dump your mates;

Sell up the Charger;

Never go to the footy;

'Cause in that sixty seconds I realised that I truly, madly, deeply, love this joint.

Put down the dog (explain that one to the kids);

Strike yourself from the electoral roll (taking your hand well and truly off the tiller of this great nation);

Throw the 'Castle' on the market;

Pack up all your favourite shit (this includes storing your least favourite shit at your mum's, and I say mum's because that's who you'd ask, you wouldn't try it on Dad, because you're an Australian, and like all other Australians your dad's 'hard' and would rather stick that three piece velour lounge suite up your arse than have it cluttering up his garage);

Not catch the waft of a thousand brick barbies on a summery Sunday arvo;

Never again seeing the look of pride on the Clearasil clean face of an eighteen-year-old 'Boyracer', whose throaty twin system V8 can just be heard under the rhythmically thumping bass speakers of his 'more expensive than the car' sound system as he endlessly cruises the main street of any Two Pub town you'd like to name;

To never again experience the rag-tag platoon

of local kids on an expedition to the creek, taking great care not to fall down any exposed drains or lose their jumper and three layers of skin to the hungry talons of the blackberry bush?

What price is paid to never feel the windy whack on the back of your skull at the whim of an angry magpie?

What about a few coldies in a beer garden with the last rays of the sun playing on your blood red back?

Or the exhilaration of taking a flying one-handed catch off the garage roof in a head-to-head struggle on the field of backyard cricket?

Or at dusk the haunting chorus of weary mothers summoning their offspring to return home from the far-flung reaches of the suburb with the promise 'TEA'S READY'?

Yep, you can hear that 'Tea's ready' anywhere, boy, those voices carry, I swear I heard them from half a world away ...

'Sorry I can't stay, I think my tea's ready.'

LINDA JAIVIN

FISH

I was sewing fish into the curtains at my ex-boyfriend's place when my mobile rang. It was him. 'Oh, g'day, Tony,' I said coolly, squeezing the phone between my shoulder and chin so that I could continue stitching. 'What do you want? I thought we weren't allowed to have any contact with each other for a month so that I could — how did you put it? — ah yes, "chill out". And what was that other phrase you used? "Get a perspective on things?" That's right.'

He wanted his key back. Typical. 'What, don't you trust me?' I answered blithely, pulling another glaze-eyed sardine out of the pail and positioning it in the unpicked hem of the fabric. A thin stream of cloudy water ran off the fish and dribbled onto his pillow. Aaaaw. Too bad. I smiled.

A plane flew overhead. He asked where I was. His house was under the flight path. Mine wasn't. Nyah nyah nyah nyah nyah. But this was not the appropriate time to gloat. 'At Sue's,' I lied. Sue was the friend who introduced us in the first place. Different suburb, same sound effects. That was a good answer. He wouldn't like the sound of me being with Sue one bit. He'd imagine we were talking about him. He'd think I was having one of my 'outbursts', as he called them.

I could hear him take a deep breath. In that deliberately calm voice I often heard him use with his more difficult patients, he said, 'It's not a matter of trust, Stephanie. It's what happens when you split up with someone. You return their key. Simple as that.'

Nothing simple about it, I thought, slipping a herring into the space next to the sardine. I picked up my needle and cotton and started to sew. I examined my handiwork. I'd done a fairly neat job. For a psychiatrist, Tony was pretty unobservant. If it took him as long to notice the bulge in the curtains as it had for him to realise that Judy, the woman he'd been fucking behind my back, was up the duff, then the fish would have plenty of time to come to term as well. 'Sorry, Tony,' I answered after a silence. 'I was so angry with you that I drove down to Bronte, found that place on the rocks where we used to sit and watch the sunset, and chucked the key into the ocean.'

He asked me if I felt good about that. Psy-fucken-chiatrists. They always ask you questions like that. 'No, I don't,' I replied sweetly. 'Some dolphin's probably choking on it as we speak. I'd much rather you were choking on it.'

He informed me that I didn't really mean that. Oh, all right, then. You know best. I didn't really mean that. I rolled my eyes and weighed a piece of cod fillet in my hand. While he reminded me of all the good times we'd allegedly shared, I attempted to slip the fish into the external disk drive on his power Mac. It wouldn't fit. Mobiles are so handy. As he continued to explain to me what I was feeling, I went into the kitchen to fetch a sharp knife. Back in the bedroom, his desk did nicely for a carving board. When I'd done with the computer, I fed the rest of the fillet and some whitebait to his CD player. It was one of those fancy ones with slots for five discs. It took quite a lot of fish.

Tony was sighing now. It was an emotionless sigh. I could tell. Tony was the sort of guy who kept in touch with his feelings by sending a card at Christmas.

He said that he had needed more freedom to move, that he'd felt confined within our relation-ship. Then he emphasised that this was his problem, not mine.

'I love it when men say that,' I responded, sliding open his underwear drawer. 'Not.' I then imitated his voice: '"It's my problem, not yours." Has it ever occurred to you how stunningly disempowering that is?' I asked him. 'It's like, the woman doesn't even have the right to claim her part of the problem. Admit it, Tony,' I demanded, wiping the knife on his briefs and then filleting them. 'It's my problem too.' So, he needed

He asked me if I felt good about that. Psy-fucken-chiatrists. They always ask you questions like that. 'No, I don't,' I replied sweetly.

more freedom to move? I knew exactly which part of him needed its freedom and I was more than happy to liberate it from its confines. I tossed the little circles of crotch material into the bucket of fish. 'It's my problem too, Tony.'

'I have often advised you to get some help,' he replied evenly. 'You tend to get a bit obsessive about things. It's not healthy.'

Obsessive? Moi? I was speechless.

I hauled the bucket of fish into the lounge. I stuffed a mackerel or two under the cushions on the sofa, put a bit of whitebait down his bong, and chucked the rest over the carpet at random.

Then I pulled the magnet from my purse and ran it carefully over the television. He was saying something about me being unbalanced, but I didn't quite catch it because I'd briefly put the phone down while tipping some metal filings under the glass plate of the microwave.

Picking up the phone again, I asked him whether his notion of balance had to do with having two lovers to play off one another. Silence.

'As if I wouldn't have found out,' I tsk-tsked. 'Judy is, after all, my own secretary.' I pulled a can of No-frills catfood — tuna flavour — out of my bag and looked for the opener.

I couldn't catch what he said next because the line suddenly went fuzzy. When it cleared, he explained he was on his mobile too. He was in the car on his way home. I looked at my watch.

'You know what really disappoints me?' I asked, striding over to the designer retro dial phone in the lounge and unscrewing the mouthpiece. I'd have to work really fast now. 'That you always said you'd be here for me. Come thick or thin. But now that things have come thick, so to speak, you're outta here.' My voice cracked.

'I can't talk to you about all this now,' Tony said, 'you're too emotional.'

'Too emotional for what?' I asked. 'You never could talk to me.' A tear welled in my eye. I wiped it on my sleeve. I told myself to get a grip. I spooned catfood into the receiver, packed it down and replaced the mouthpiece. Then I dialled the number of a telephone dominatrix service in San Francisco and left the phone off the hook. 'You refuse to acknowledge you have any emotions at all,' I accused. 'You're on permanent emote control.'

'Are you trying to provoke me?' he asked evenly.

'Now why would I do that?' I took stock. I probably wouldn't have time to shave or crazy-colour the dog or Vegemite the door handles. But things don't always work out according to plan. As I shook out a live eel into the washing machine, I heard a car pull up the drive. Shit. 'Look, Tony, I can't talk now. Have a nice life, okay?' I hung up, grabbed my bag and dashed out the back door. Tossing the key in the compost, I snuck around the side of the house to peep at the drive.

Phew.

Judy poked her head out from the cab. 'Mission accomplished?' she asked.

'Yup,' I said, swinging my bag into the boot and giving her the thumbs up. A plane flew overheard. We both looked up. We smiled at each other. I took her hand and we kissed. 'Airport, please,' I said to the driver.

ROY SLAVEN

TRAINING ROOTING KING

Over the years many people, close and not so close to the racing game, have asked me how I would prepare Rooting King for a big race and until now I have been unwilling to disclose the information for obvious reasons. Rooting King was what I would call a personality horse — he could be helpful, wistful, engaging, endearing and funny one day, and be a sulking, petulant idiot the next, and so to meet these extreme personality demands I embarked on a training regimen that made no allowances for his personality. In short, it was important that it be abundantly clear that I was the boss and The King was the bunny.

When a race of interest was looming I would start routine work two weeks from the off. Without warning I would thunder into his stable early and brandish the whip. Then I'd go outside and let him think about it for a few hours. Then I'd go back in and show him the whip again. Then I'd leave him to stew for a day. Let's say the first brandishing of the whip was a Monday, then on Wednesday morning at a quarter to five I'd get him out on the track and race him flat out for about fifteen kilometres. Then I'd put him back, hose him off, give him some oats and play some Slade very loudly for an hour. This routine I would keep up for five days. I found that 'Cum On Feel The Noise' on a continuous loop could put the King in a state of mind where it was best to give him a very wide berth. But it was a state of mind essential to his racing, and it was a state of mind that I liked.

On day eight I'd have him up early and give him a hose, then put him back.

Day nine up early, a hose and a ride in the special float I'd designed. This float was of such a style as to be attached to the front of the Ford with the door section of the float removed so that he could feel the breeze and see the road. The float floor was lowered to within six millime-

He was allowed to root for much of the day until about four in the afternoon when he had a Bowen Method massage and a saline spa.

tres of the road and I'd travel at about 180ks. This was to give him a feeling for speed. Once or twice I might brake suddenly and watch him career off into the distance at great speed. When I did this he would often manage to stay on his feet. Other times he would fall over, look really ungainly, and end up disappearing around a bend on his back, or career off into the bush to be brought up short by a large gum tree. But I think, in the main, he probably enjoyed it. He never once baulked at getting into the special float. But I wouldn't recommend this for horses with dicky ankles. Mercifully The King had ankles like iron-bark. Again I'd hose him off and put him back.

Day ten I'd run him in the middle of the day until he was choking on foam. This would tell me how fit he was. If he started foaming badly after an hour I'd know he was underdone. Usually he'd start gagging after about three hours. Then I'd hose out his mouth, give him a spin in the float for an hour and put him away. Fifteen minutes later I'd repeat the process.

Day eleven I'd ignore him.

Day twelve was

Was The King a vegetarian? The answer is no. The King liked nothing more than a nice piece of pickled pork, or a brisket or some very fatty forequarter always earmarked for sprint work. We'd start with five metre sprints (200 of them), then fifteen metre sprints (100), and finish off with two thousand metre sprints (8). Then a hose and back in.

Day thirteen was always the day The King liked best. He was allowed to root for much of the day until about four in the afternoon when he had a Bowen Method massage and a saline spa.

Day fourteen was race day. I'd wake The King as late as possible and spend a quiet few moments with him, showing him photographs of past wins and playing him recordings of Ken Callendar and Johnnie Tapp calling the last few furlongs of past victories. Then it was into the conventional float with a bale of hay, a salt-lick and some molasses for the journey to either Flemington or Randwick.

The other question I've been most asked over the years concerning The King is his diet. Was The King a vegetarian? The answer is no. The King liked nothing more than a nice piece of pickled pork, or a brisket or some very fatty forequarter short loin lamb chops. That's not to say that he didn't like vegetables, far from it, he could wolf down all manner of legume or squash or leaf. But for speed and distance and a seriously competitive frame of mind, meat was always an essential part of his diet.

Needless to say if The King won, which he did on more than eighty-two percent of occasions over a seventeen year career, he was treated very well. The paddock was his to loll about in for nearly a month with every form of sexual whim gratified and all dietary needs catered for. If he lost, he would work underground in the Genders coal mine in Lithgow dragging slag in skips for a few weeks to cool his heels.

Training, then, is very simple. Just get to know the horse and the rest is easy. As I tell kiddies in clinics every day, the important thing is to make training fun for yourself and an absolute physical and emotional nightmare for the horse. And I know for a fact that Bart and TJ and Lee and Sugarlips and Gai would agree.

H G NELSON

RIDING ROOTING KING

Rooting King was an evil, uncontrollable horse. The big rangy chestnut was almost impossible to ride. But 'The Damp Sock', as the stable called him, loved to race. For any jockey legged aboard The Sock, it was not so much a ride but a wild and rowdy contact with the grim reaper in club colours.

I first met Rooting King when I was a young hoop just making my mark on the rich Barossa Valley circuit in the late sixties. I knew nothing of The Sock's fearsome reputation. I was a green mug. I had no idea that jockeys across the nation refused to ride the bugger.

The King was road freighted into town for a hit-and-run mission with The Nuriootpa Pillow his main focus. The Pillow was the last race on the Barossa Valley Cup eight race card. Rooting King's trainer, Roy Slaven, had set the horse for The Pillow after his showing in The Lithgow Stool, where he flashed home for an eye-catching be-on-me-next-time seventh.

... and a kick to the cruets which was already on the swell, drawing attention to the trouser in the most attractive manner.

I had a full book of rides on the Cup day card and knew most of the horses personally. Only The King was a mystery to me.

When I didn't know a horse I used to introduce myself by riding to the course with them in the horse float. I used to get in for a bit of a fiddle with the mount. I have always maintained that races were won or lost in the float. I had no idea when I slipped into the track-bound float that The King hated humans. He rightly saw humans as bludging, two-legged types who made him do things he didn't want to and inflicted pain.

The horse went off as soon as he caught a whiff. It is true in those days I packed a pretty powerful wallop on the aroma front. The trip from stables to track took a mere fifteen minutes. I was tipped out on course a complete mess.

Luckily Roy's stable chief, Ed 'The Shed'

Tinsel, had done a first aid course with the St Johns Ambulance. He quickly got me on my feet and on top of my condition. He diagnosed a dislocated finger on a broken wrist, an arm knocked from the collarbone, unspecified internal bleeding and a kick to the cruets which was already on the swell, drawing attention to the trouser in the most attractive manner.

The horse emerged from the gloom as fresh as a daisy. The Shed said later he swore he saw a smile flicker across The King's lips.

Before passing out I bellowed at The Shed, 'For God's sake Tinsel, don't tell Roy I'm crook!' The Shed fixed me up as best he could with applications of those great trainer's tools, the sugar bag full of hot sand and the freezing cold bag of party ice. With these two applied to the groin bruising in rotation you soon lose all feeling and with a sniff of the smelling salts you come round feeling tickety-boo.

I gritted my teeth and strolled out to the mounting enclosure as the horses began circulating. The course looked an absolute picture with Barossa begonias on the bloom and a record crowd on hand to see The Cup, the feature race of the spring carnival.

Roy met me for final instructions. I said nothing. I couldn't. I was hurting too much to chat. It was an agonising effort just being in the perpendicular. Roy gave me a final spray. In those days, before his media appearances had smoothed the rough edges, Roy was a wild man of racing, a sort of early cross between Bill Waterhouse and George Freeman. He gave me a real serve about how to ride the horse. 'Get him out early, Pal. He is a deadset bludger and he needs a belt. Are you listening to me, Sport? Whack him hard and keep whacking. Don't stop whacking until you are back here. Okay! Now off you shoot and win!'

Ed legged me aboard gingerly. I gritted my teeth, biting down on a copy of TJ Smith's biography. I felt like a loser and looked like a joke. The hooter birds were on the blow as I took the horse out onto the track.

As the field in The Pillow was boxed, the money came later for the fancied two, Princess Pants Off and Planet Tooler, with the Bart Cummings trained Sir Spun Cave on the next line of betting at three to one.

My teeth were connected directly by a wire to the horse's love gear and it gave me an enormous sense of power.

The barrier attendants boxed The King in gate seventeen. I couldn't sit down in the saddle in that confined space. I had to take a place on the metal supports of the barrier gate itself.

My plan was to leap onto the horse as soon as they were let go. The seconds before the jump seemed like hours. I had in my teeth, along with TJ's book, a tool tugging leash that Ed had fixed up for me.

This was a simple mechanism that enabled me to communicate with the horse without a whip, as my flogging arm had carked it in the rough and tumble of the float ride. I hadn't used a tool tugger before but it seemed easy enough. My teeth were connected directly by a wire to the horse's love gear and it gave me an enormous sense of power.

The course starter, a Mr B D B Elias, let them go. I jumped off the uprights. I almost fell off, such was the sheer power as The King hit the ground running. We lost several lengths before I could get a hang of the tool tugger. It took me the first thousand metres to realise the harder I tugged the faster The King went. We were a hopeless last as the field went down the back straight.

The field packed at the top of the turn with Sir Spun Cave and Princess Pants Off setting the pace up front. Halfway down that long Nuriootpa straight I was travelling well enough to think I had a chance. I was on the tug furiously and the horse was responding to my vigour.

I loomed up on the outside of Planet Tooler, who was seventh one off the fence. The Tool always wanted to put the nip on the other horses in transit. He put a good bite on my horse. I thought that's it. But in doing so, The Tool got on the wrong leg and went wide, running into the outside running rail and ending up in the members' car park.

The crowd was on its feet screaming.

In the shadows of the post, the last thing I remember seeing was Sir Spun Cave's back door. Then it all went hazy and black. I woke up in the back of the course ambulance on my way to the base hospital. Ed said The King lunged at the post in his final stride and got up to score. I had bloused The Cave on the line.

Ed assured me I had lost none of my admirers when I fell off over the line, as I had proved The King could be ridden even when the hoop was hurting. Before lapsing back into the black, I remember Ed saying that I had the hoof print of every horse in the race on my back. The fact that the field was beginning to slow as they passed the post was the only thing that saved my life.

TREVOR MARMALADE

HOOT IN HONKERS

Life can be a funny thing, and you can quote me on that. For instance, if you had wanted to bet me six months ago that I would be standing in Tiananmen Square with Damien Oliver on my shoulders, you probably could have claimed my house.

But more of that later. The reason that I visited Hong Kong in the first place was actually due to my only ever attempt at matchmaking. Twelve years ago I lined up a couple of friends of mine, Dave and Jenny, and now they live together and have two kids. And they have both been good enough to forgive me. These days they are living in Honkers, carving out a pretty good living on the punt. And what they do between race meetings is ring up and ask when I'm coming over, to the point where it almost became 'that thing we don't mention any more'.

Pretty soon after dumping the luggage at my hotel in Wan Chai, Dave and Jen picked me up for my first dining experience in Hong Kong. For the trip there were basically two dining out jokes. When deciding where to go —

'What do you feel like?'

'I don't know ... Chinese, perhaps.'

And then when you arrive at the Chinese restaurant —

'There's a lot of locals here. That's a good sign.'

The guys and I are friendly with Melbourne Cup winning jockey, Damien Oliver, who was over there riding for David Hayes. So Oliver, or 'Oleewah' as the locals called him, joined us and he suggested that I get right into the action and stay at his place in Sha Tin, check out the stables in the morning and have a look at track work. Now normally I'm not really a morning type of person. As my old man used to say about sleep — it's the hours after midday that really count.

As it turned out I was pretty interested to see the setup there, with the horses living in high-rise stables in air-conditioned comfort. Damien was starting to have a good run after a slow start. And in Hong Kong there is nothing more important than a good start. Especially since the Australian jockeys are generally held in fairly low esteem. Michael Clarke was over there a couple of years ago and fell off at his first ride. After that he was known as 'unlucky jockey' and the punters wouldn't bet on him and the owners wouldn't put him on. Another Australian rider who had been a recent visitor was the bespectacled Peter Hutchinson. When he arrived for his first press conference wearing glasses the locals declared he was obviously no good because he couldn't see. Peter's dry Aussie sense of humour did him no favours either. He kicked a winner through on the rails at his second meeting and when interviewed afterwards about his tactics, replied that he 'just followed the white fuzzy thing'.

At sparrows' the next day we were having a good look around until Hayes' stable foreman, Almond, turned up and pointed out that no one was allowed in the stables the day before a race meeting. So Hayes whisked me up to the grandstand to watch the trials. 'There goes one of mine,' he said. 'Blazing Ballad. It will win a race while you're here.' I nodded, then disregarded it entirely, because anyone knows that trainers are absolute tipping machines. The important thing to remember when it comes to tipping is that plenty of horses have made fools of men and that men hardly ever make fools out of horses. Never, if you don't count dressage and El Caballo Blanco.

Night racing at Happy Valley on a Wednesday

is a splendid sight under lights. Within half an hour of arriving I got to see the lowest rated horse on the island win and the highest rated horse run like a busted crab. The tips were reasonably good except we loaded up on a thing called King's Glamour which did a great job to run the winner to a neck, especially considering the slaughter given to it by local rider, Simon Yim.

With a couple of days to kill before the next meeting, Jen suggested that I tag up with a mutual friend in David Brosnan who was popping up to Beijing to visit his son, Christian, who goes to uni there. And why not?

A little tip here. When applying for your Chinese visa in Hong Kong, I was told by friends not to put 'journalist' or 'dissident' down as my occupation on the application form. Not even a racing journalist is allowed in. Mind you, having met a few racing journos, this may be a matter of good taste rather than dodgy politics. Either way, I have another addition to that list. Don't put 'entertainer' on your form either. The poor woman at the China Travel Service was most perplexed by this term. She cursed, she rifled through the dictionary but it was to no avail. There is no Chinese word for entertainer. Maybe she thought I was a clown. Or even worse, a juggler. In any case, she eventually waved her arms and sent me to another branch. This time I put 'actor' because anyone knows they are harmless. The young girl there was very impressed and stamped my ticket.

Friday we took a drive to The Great Wall. We figured we may as well, since the only other place you can see it is from the moon and we weren't headed that way.

Later that night Brossie rang and asked if it was all right if Damien and a mate of his called Tommy joined us on the trip. I was about to say that it is a free world, but of course it's not, so I told him that if China had no objections then I wasn't about to overrule.

So that was the crew, and as it turned out, Tommy seemed like a top bloke, even if he did say that Trevor is a weird name. Or more precisely, 'Chewa' is a weird name. Which it probably is. As it turned out, with the Chinese having a different word for everything, Tommy and Christian came in pretty handy when it came to conversing with the locals.

We spent the day wandering through the Forbidden City, and the Summer Palace and around dusk headed for Tiananmen Square for a bit of a poke around. This was a good time to go to the square. As we arrived, the military academy which backs onto one side of the square was just cutting school for the day and it was an amazing sight to see a couple of thousand Red Army cadets pile out in formation and load up onto the trucks.

Probably the most striking feature of Tiananmen Square, apart from Mao's portrait, is the gigantic digital clock counting down the seconds until the June 30 takeover of Hong Kong. I saw Tommy staring at it and asked what he thought. He said, 'Well, Chewa, we haven't got one of those in Hong Kong.'

Over on the Mao's mausoleum side of the square there were a few hundred people gathered around a pole for the trooping of the flag. As I'm standing on tippy toes to get a look, I feel two hands on my shoulders. 'I want to get a photo, Trev. Jockey up!' And there I was. In Tiananmen Square with Damien Oliver on my shoulders. At this point I figured from the amusement of the locals that this may have been a breach of etiquette. At least one day I can tell my grand-children that I was ridden by a Melbourne Cup winner. Even if Damien did say I was badly in need of the run.

Friday we took a drive to The Great Wall. We figured we may as well, since the only other place you can see it is from the moon and we weren't headed that way. And they did go to a fair bit of trouble over it. 'Class one wall,' said Tommy.

Possibly the most amazing thing was that after

climbing a couple of thousand steps and squeezing through a few gates, we got to the top and there was a hundred-year-old guy with a camel. How do they get a fucking camel up there? All we can figure is that the guy was there when they built it and volunteered to stay back and hustle a buck out of tourists.

After watching our driver get slapped around a bit for parking in a no-standing zone, we headed off for our Beijing dining experience. Tommy and Christian did all of the ordering, which turned out to be delicacies such as barbecued pigeon and goose's feet. I reneged on the rat with wings and what can I tell you about the goose foot? They sort of shell them like a prawn, so what you get is rubbery on the outside and a bit crunchy in the middle.

'Yeah, there's small bits of cartilage in there,' said Christian. It's quite uncanny how full one feels after that.

Another little tip. If you ever have to catch a plane out of Beijing, there are two ways of avoiding the queues at the airport. Either get there three hours before your flight or about half an hour after it was supposed to leave. This is because a Jumbo holding about four hundred people has two people checking them through at the desk. And it's hard to wonder what the excuse is. Not enough people to choose from? The reality is that anyone that can speak a bit of

English is working as a prostitute or a waiter at KFC. That's where the real money is.

Back in Honkers on Sunday and the race meeting is at Sha Tin, which is a real racetrack in the mould of Flemington or Randwick.

At some stage the previous night I must have decided that turning up with a raging hangover may improve my luck. After eight glasses of 7-Up, I had a launch at the buffet, which was very well turned out by the Hong Kong Club. What is it about a buffet? I mean, when was the last time you were at a restaurant and said to the waiter, 'I'll have three slices of rare roast beef, some rice topped with chicken curry, some pasta with beef stroganoff, four prawns, half-a-dozen oysters, potato salad, some smoked salmon, some ham, and a couple of slices of hot salami. And I want it all at once on the same plate.'

Outside things didn't get much better. Hayes trained a treble, but hadn't thought any of them could win. One of the winners was a horse called Premiership, ridden by Damien Oliver, who also forgot to mention that it had a chance. And of course Blazing Ballad ran about sixth. By this time I figured that I should catch up with the boys because it was obviously their shout.

'Did you back Premiership?' said Hayes, clutching at straws.

'No,' I said. 'Were you tipping it?'

'I thought you might have backed it because of

North Melbourne winning the flag.'

'What? Like an omen bet? Good on you.'

Maybe I should have brought my girlfriend. She would have backed it. Not me, though. I'm far too smart for that. At least I saved my money on the Tiananmen Square thing.

SANTO CILAURO

WRESTLING WITH FACT AND FANTASY

When I was little, my parents forgot to teach me English. At the age of four, I uttered my first non-Italian words: 'Zig' and 'Zag'. Revenge on my mother and father was cruel — every day, for hours on end, I would march up and down the corridor and chant, 'You and me, we will be partners. You and me, we will be pals. You and me, we will be partners. You and me, we will be pals. You and me, we will be partners ... '

But television was more than just my first English teacher. By the time I was in Grade 4, it began testing the processes of my inner mind. The first complex philosophical issue I ever dealt with was 'Who was the better Stooge, Curly or Shemp?'

When this fiery schoolyard debate reached its third consecutive lunchtime, I began feeling disconcerted about something else — to my horror, I realised there were some kids in my grade who confessed they *weren't allowed* to watch 'The Three Stooges' because their parents thought it was too violent. They could only watch weird stuff like 'Doctor Who'. I felt sorry for them.

Then I got to thinking — perhaps my own welfare was being neglected. I immediately questioned my father on the ideological soundness of not only *allowing* me to watch, idolise, and imitate three demented clowns but actually *encouraging* me to do so. 'Shut up,' he answered, 'I'm watching the wrestling.'

The wrestling. That one, all-pervading omnipresent image from my early life — a purely televisual image — so much so, that whenever I went to Festival Hall to see it live, it seemed totally unreal.

The wrestling. Pronounced 'Dha ressolin'. No one told me Santa Claus didn't exist. No one told me about the facts of life. But when I was old enough, a delegation comprising three uncles and a godfather took me aside for the ancient initiation ritual of telling me that the wrestling was fake.

Here is an excerpt from that conversation (I could get a curse for revealing this):

Uncle*: Ey, boy, the wrestling is rigged.

Me: (Pause) Yeah, so?

Uncle: (Hitting me) So, shut up and don't tell your grandmother.

My grandmother was a great wrestling fan. Despite being a staunch believer that man walking on the moon was a staged event, the woman maintained that the wrestling was real. She was particularly fond of the midgets. 'Look! The dwarf just ran under the referee's legs! This is funnier than Jerry Lewis.'

Once, an Indian wrestler called Tiger Singh got booed and had stuff thrown at him by hundreds of Greek and Italian spectators just because he knelt down in his corner to perform some Hindu prayers. 'It's not fair,' I thought. 'He shouldn't get

Da-da-dum, dum-dum. Kshh! Da-da-dum, dum-dum. Kshh ...!'

hassled because of his religion.'

It dawned on me that the worst form of racism is that which emanates from the victims of racism. When I told this to my uncle, he hit me.

Watching 'World Championship Wrestling' was a ritual in itself. Every Sunday just before midday the television would be tuned to Channel Nine where B A Santamaria would be signing off from his mystifying program, 'Point of View'.

This was the standard greeting he'd get from our family:

Cousin: Get off, you bald bastard, we want wrestling!

Uncle: (Hitting him) Shut up, he's Italian.

When the WCW theme started, we all sang along even though it didn't have any words. 'Da-da-dum, dum-dum. Kshh! Da-da-dum, dum-dum. Kshh ...!'

A special treat for the non-English speakers in our lounge room was when commentator Jack Little interviewed Italian wrestlers after their bouts.

Little: Mario, how about a few words to our Italian friends?

Mario Milano: (Translated) Come see me next week when I will break Abdullah the Butcher's neck! I would also like to wish all of you a happy and peaceful Easter.

The hour of wrestling would fly by and before we knew it, Jack Little would be yelling the words 'Next Saturdee Night at Fesss-tival Hall!!!' far too close to the microphone.

We'd still be badmouthing Waldo Von Erich and his Nazi tendencies (my uncle claims to have fought in the war with him), when suddenly my grandfather would shut us up. 'Hey! Quit it! 'Roller Derby' is on!' Great, more wrestling — only with roller-skates. That was followed by Epic Theatre — more wrestling — only with sandals ...

Nowadays, I don't watch as much TV as I used to, but occasionally — in my quieter moments — I ask myself the question: 'Who was the better Stooge, Curly or Shemp?'

* Not a real uncle. 'Uncle: Anyone allowed to hit you with his belt.'

SANTO CILAURO

THE DOG FORMERLY KNOWN AS 'PRINCE'

Every dog my grandfather ever had was called 'Prince' (except a girl dog that he called 'Princess'). They were all tough dogs. He only fed them bread with milk in the morning and bones at night and sometimes leftover spaghetti. He loved all his dogs very much even though sometimes he'd whip them with the hose.

I only knew the last two Princes.

1969
The second-last Prince was already old when I was born. He loved me very much and would bite any person who tried to hit me — which in an Italian house, was anyone.

Both my parents used to go to work early in the morning, so my grandfather and Prince would take me to school. One day when Prince

47

was seventeen and I was seven, my grandfather came to pick me up but there was no Prince with him. 'Dov'è Prince?' I asked — that means 'Where's Prince?' (my English wasn't very good when I was in Grade 2). He wouldn't tell me. I insisted, so he took me to the intersection of Gold Street and Alexander Parade. Near the grill on the gutter was a mat of bloody black fur and pink sausagey-looking stuff. 'Li è Prince' ('There is Prince'). He said it like he was saying 'There is a traffic light'. It was the first time I went to school without Prince.

The reason he didn't drop the ball is because it wasn't one. It was another dog's ear stuck in his tooth.

1973

Despite having a combined height of 4' 8", Trio and I used to play 'rucks' in the backyard every day after school. We would throw a plastic football up onto the roof and wait for it to roll down. I'd be Len Thompson and he'd be Bob Heard (not once did we stop and question why two ruckmen from the same team would ever want to contest each other). You got two points if you got a clear tap out, and four points if you hit the rover with it. The rover was the new Prince. One day I managed to get the ball down in the

Prince-direction, who in turn rolled it straight into a box of prickly pears. They ended up scattering all over the place.

At that moment, we all heard my grandfather's whistle — he used to do that halfway down the street so everyone knew he was about to come home and get scared. When Prince heard that sound, he got scared. In a moment of panic, he tried to push all the prickly pears back into the box with his nose. Prickly pears are called prickly pears because they have prickles all over them — by the time my grandfather got to the end of the driveway, Prince's face looked like a voodoo doll.

1976

When we played cricket on the street, Prince used to field in the covers. Unfortunately, we played on the corner of Ballarat and Hotham Streets so covers was on a pretty busy road. As a consequence, he got knocked over four times — once by a semitrailer. Despite this, he never lost his enthusiasm for fielding. One day, we decided to play with a cork ball. He broke a tooth when he took a catch to dismiss Perry Papas.

1978

Once, Prince came home with something in his mouth. I thought it was a ball so I said, 'Drop the ball, Prince.' He didn't. So I said 'Drop the ball' again. Again, he didn't. The reason he didn't drop the ball is because it wasn't one. It was another dog's ear stuck in his tooth.

1983
When I didn't live in Collingwood anymore, I used to drop in on my grandfather every morning on the way to university. Prince would always wait for me on the verandah at quarter past eight.

One morning, he wasn't on the verandah. Because he was old, I figured that he'd died. I came in and asked my grandfather if Prince was dead. He didn't think so although he hadn't seen him since the day before. We went into the shed where Prince lived and we saw him shivering under the tool bench. There was no light so we couldn't see him properly. When we pulled him out, we saw that he was completely covered in coagulated blood. After we hosed him down, we realised someone had tried to cut his head off with a knife. 'It's the Aboriginal kids down the street. I've seen them throwing bricks at him,' my grandfather said. He then poured half a bottle of methylated spirits onto the gash. I said I'd take him to the vet. 'No dog of mine will ever go to the vet!' yelled my grandfather, like he was saying 'No wife of mine will ever go to work!' But I took him anyway. The vet said we'd have to put him down. But I disagreed and told him how tough Prince was. The vet eventually agreed to stitch him up but after about a day, the wound opened up and pus started coming out. The vet said 'I told you so', but I said it was because he only put in six stitches. So this time, he put in about twenty-five. It worked. The only problem was that the wound was so big and he'd put in so many stitches, that Prince's skin got pulled really taut. He looked Chinese — you could only just see his eyes at the bottom of his eye slits.

My grandfather would be so ashamed if he knew his dog is the only dog in history to have had a facelift.

STEVE BEDWELL

BITS AND PIECES

MOVIES I DIDN'T LIKE

I didn't like *Jaws* because I'm scared of sharks.

I didn't like *The Towering Inferno* because I was once in a fire.

I didn't like *The Poseidon Adventure* because I've been on a boat that sank.

I didn't like *The Crying Game* because ... it doesn't matter why! ... I just didn't, okay!

MY NANNA

My nanna represented Australia at the Berlin Olympics.

My nanna held two world records.

My nanna won everything on 'Pick-a-box'.

My nanna rode a pushbike from Sydney to Perth.

The day my nanna forgot her name, dad bunged her into a home.

THINGS THAT KIDS WILL NEVER LEARN

People know when you're letting them win.

The teacher can always tell if you did your homework on the bus.

The best way to get a budgie is to start out by asking for a horse.

Don't wear it if it itches.

Even if you make a really nice place for it to live, with sticks and dirt and grass, a praying mantis will still spend all of its time trying to get out of the jar.

Bruce Beresford

FAMILY TREE

He insisted he stay on in the house in the country after our mother died. 'You'll never get him out,' friends said to me, 'they never want to let go even though they'd be much better off in a retirement home.' This was, sadly, true, even though my sister and I visited a number of places and then took him the brochures along with improbable stories of the wonderful time he was going to have with all the other old people.

We weren't being entirely selfish. He did very little work around the house or large garden when our energetic mother was alive and I saw no reason for an onslaught of activity. I doubted if he was capable of cooking anything at all. As a small child, on the rare occasions our mother was away for a few days, he fed my sister and me on chips. Cut very thick. Cooked in lashings of oil.

For every meal. I recall being delighted at the time.

'What will you do all day?' my sister demanded. He spluttered and rambled, trotting out his usual array of unfinished sentences, though the tone was unmistakable — *no pioneer home*. I knew what he'd do all day. Just as he'd always done, but more of it. If there was no cricket or AFL on the television, an amble across to the general store, down to the tourist souvenir shop, and/or up the hill to the local pub (now smartened up and run by a couple of young men from Paddington) where he would bore anyone he could find with half-remembered and incoherently presented stories of his life as a travelling washing machine salesman in the thirties. True, there were a few local friends but I suspected they were more the friends of our mother, and would now take evasive action. Perhaps there were already none left. Most were reliant on Zimmer frames and given to dying on the bowling green or while sipping cups of tea as a TV newsreader described events in a world they had long since ceased to understand.

The first time I visited after her death — it must have been a couple of months as I'd been away working — I was amazed at the changes, even though I had foreseen them. The grass had grown up and either choked or hidden all my mother's flowers. The front door was jammed shut and I noticed there was glass all over the porch. The porch light cover had been broken. Convinced the poor old codger had been attacked and robbed I walked around the side of the house and pushed aside the pendulous passionfruit that hung down over the kitchen door. The kitchen smelt and was filthy, with empty baked bean tins all over the floor and sink. (There were no dirty plates as he ate directly from the tins.) The living room had wet clothes strewn over the sofas and mushrooms growing in the carpet. Newspapers were piled everywhere, thousands of them. He'd hoarded them all his life, but my mother had succeeded in keeping them out of the house, apart from a pile in the bedroom, with the result that the garage was so full of them there was no possibility of using it for the car. The odd thing was that, although he bought all of them every day, I could never recall him reading anything in them except the sports pages. There was no point in mentioning to him any catastrophe, revolution, political event, murder, or robbery. He'd never heard of it. (He was evidently taken by complete surprise at the outbreak of the Second World War but somehow successfully resisted induction into the army, managing to spend the war, he told me once, as 'a Sussex Street commando'. I used to boast about this to my school friends, until I found out from a much-decorated uncle that it was an office job.) If any effort was made to remove any of the newspapers, even the pre-war ones, he resisted vigorously, proclaiming 'there's an article in one of them I want to read.'

Now he sat in front of the TV wearing an old and bean-stained dressing-gown, watching the cricket, 'G'day,' he said, 'look at this. Richards, my godfather, he can hit. Look, he ... like Keith Miller. Remember when we saw Miller? ... Lots of ... ' Yes, I replied, we'd seen Miller lots of times at the Sydney Cricket Ground. Being burnt to a crisp at the cricket ground, while the agonisingly slow games drifted on day after day, was the main thing we'd done together. He didn't respond much to anything else, certainly not my schoolwork. I don't think he even found out I'd been to university, though his interest in films perked up slightly when I became a director. We even went to a few movies, though the plots and characters all baffled him; they'd become so much more complicated since the days of Errol Flynn and Ronald Coleman. After their deaths his interest in movies had lapsed.

I stayed with him a few days. I opened all the windows to let some air in and get rid of the dankness. He shut them all again. I found him showering fully dressed — except for his shoes — so that he could wash his clothes as well as his body. He said it saved time. I said he didn't need to save time and he should use the washing machine ... I couldn't even persuade him to hang the wet clothes outside. He continued to drape them over the sofa and was happy to wear them soggy. I took him out shopping and for some meals in the local town, about thirty minutes away down the mountain. He was angry because I wouldn't let him drive the car. He'd always been an appalling driver and had lost his licence a number of times, not that this had prevented him from driving even for one day. On the bridge over the Hawkesbury I pointed out

Why would they be sitting among chicken bones under the front seat of an old Holden instead of in the bank?

to him that this was where he'd missed the turn and gone into the river with my mother and aunt as passengers. They'd all been rescued, in the middle of the night, by some American tourists. He scoffed at this proof of his incompetence, just as he snorted and avoided my attempts at involving him in a discussion — as a prelude to reintroducing the subject of the retirement village — of the run-down house, ridiculous diet, or even the fact he'd never changed a light bulb, but was content to sit in the dark, and then find his way from room to room with a torch.

A couple of smart little restaurants had opened, all cappuccino, goat cheese and focaccia. He walked past these, insisting on Kentucky Fried Chicken. I protested, but had to give in. Almost anything was better than the baked beans. Was I imagining it, or were people walking towards us suddenly crossing the street? He waved (he'd lived in the district for years and knew almost everyone) and called to them effusively, though they managed to scamper away, intent on appointments to right and left. Only one poor old lady on a Zimmer frame lacked the necessary speed so was cornered and told about my career. How I had always been obsessed with films etc, etc, etc. He raved on and on to the poor old thing, skilfully blocking her feeble efforts to inch away from him. I doubt if she'd seen a film since the days of Pearl White and had no idea what this 'Director' could possibly do. Didn't actors make up the stories?

We ate the chicken in the car parked down by the river. He wouldn't get out and sit at one of the picnic tables. After he'd died, a couple of years later, I picked up the old car and, when cleaning it out, found he'd been in the habit of stuffing his Kentucky Fried chicken bones under the front seat. There were hundreds of them, along with three medical benefit cheques payable to him after my mother's illness and totalling over $5000. Why would they be sitting among chicken bones under the front seat of an old Holden instead of in the bank? What could have prompted him to put them there, especially as he needed the money?

As I lay in bed, in the damp sheets, I consoled myself with the thought that at least he didn't drink. Only an occasional beer. He could have been in this tumbledown house, with baked beans and no light in an alcoholic stupor. Then he could fall through the big picture window right down the mountain, or drive the car back into the river.

I phoned my sister and told her I couldn't even involve him in a conversation about moving, let alone get his agreement. The visit depressed me, not really because of him, but for all the memories of my mother. I hunted through an old chest for some pictures of her. There were only two or three. In one of them she was seventeen years old, her face unlined, her dark hair pulled back severely in the fashion of the time, her eyes sparkling with joy and youth and optimism.

I didn't see him again for over a year. I went to America to make a film. I called him a few days after arriving back in Sydney. I couldn't face the house again and suggested he come down and stay with me.

'You took the car keys with you,' he said, accusingly.

'It's not a good idea for you to drive. You can get the train down.'

'You come up here. There's someone I want you to meet.'

'Not if you're going to tell everyone we run across that I'm a film director.'

'Why are you going on about that again? What does it ... '

'It embarrasses me.'

I thought I'd better face up to it and check out the house. Maybe I could arrange for a gardener and cleaner. I'd sent some there already but he'd sent them away again saying, despite overwhelming evidence to the contrary, that he had no problem maintaining the house or garden. He asked me who was in the film I'd done. I named four famous actors but he'd never heard of any of them. They were all post-Errol Flynn. He was impressed, though, that Hurd Hatfield played a minor part. I'd never understood why, but he'd always been an admirer of *The Picture of Dorian Gray*, a 1945 film that was Hurd's sole claim to fame. Was it Hatfield's good looks that appealed to him? Old photographs showed my father as handsome and slim when young. I knew he'd imagined himself as the movie-star type and had even worked as an extra in some Australian films of the thirties. No doubt his acting career suffered through the same lack of application that characterised everything he did. Or was it the story of the transference of guilt to a painting that appealed? I still vividly remember the visits to various girlfriends when he was a commercial traveller (Bodega wines succeeded the washing machines) and I, as a very small boy, would be left for hours sitting in a parked car outside city apartment buildings or suburban houses. I remember, too, the screaming matches and weeping apologies when my mother found out about some of these liaisons, no doubt because he showed no more skill at deceit and subterfuge than he did at anything else.

As I drove toward the mountains I compiled in my head a list of the bizarre rules he'd imposed in my childhood, all of them accepted at the time, most of them only questioned when I was in high school and came into contact with the families of school friends, causing me to query previously held tenets of 'normal' behaviour. We weren't allowed to wear shoes in the house, even visitors had to take them off at the front door. The radio was never to be switched on. At one point, and for some years, we had to be in our pyjamas at 4.30 pm and in bed by 6.00 pm — humiliating for a ten year old whose friends were all out in the street playing cricket. All pets were banned as they kept him awake at night. He even bought a rifle and shot neighbours' animals as they strayed into our yard, a pastime that did not endear me to the local kids. No one was allowed to talk at the dinner table, but had to point to anything that was wanted. Sundays were the worst. He wanted to 'have a little lie-in' and invariably did so until three in the afternoon. My sister and I were not allowed to get out of bed on this day until we heard him moving around the house.

At one point, and for some years, we had to be in our pyjamas at 4.30 pm and in bed by 6.00 pm ...

'You see,' said my father, his voice tense with excitement, 'Herb is a direct descendant of Jesus Christ.'

I thought of my own children and how much easier their lives are. How hard I tried to make their childhoods more fun than mine had been. But ... if one of them were writing this, how would I be portrayed? I've had hints from them, intercepted glances during conversations, that imply I am not the reasonable and amiable father I imagine myself to be.

He wouldn't tell me who he wanted me to meet but pushed me back out to the car almost immediately, clearly anxious to avoid any conversation about the further deterioration of the house, which now looked like a set for a Hammer horror. I drove back down the mountain, then along a dirt road that went for miles alongside the river, past old farmhouses and an occasional health farm or camping site. Finally, we went up a driveway towards a run-down but attractive double storeyed brick house built in the mid-nineteenth century, not exactly restored but well maintained.

Herb Gillespie was a stocky man in his late fifties, weathered and brown from a life lived outdoors, though with a smooth face, devoid of life's experiences, as is often found among nuns or the retarded. As we shook hands in his kitchen he took off his hat to reveal an almost completely bald head. I noticed that his eyes were unnaturally bright and of no real colour, just that of an empty bottle. My father seemed very excited at the introduction.

'Herb's got something to show you,' he said, his voice assuming a reverential tone that puzzled me. He led the way into the living room, which someone had furnished in the twenties and never altered since. I was admiring some of the pieces when my father indicated I should look to the wall. Herb gestured toward a large chart that was hanging there. I went closer. It was a genealogy chart of some sort, but one with far more rambling ramifications than the one I remembered from school about the kings of England.

'You see,' said my father, his voice tense with excitement, 'Herb is a direct descendant of Jesus Christ.'

'Oh ... yes ... of course,' I said, glancing across at Herb, who smiled slightly at me in a self-deprecating kind of way, though his eyes seemed to have an extra glint. I thought it might be prudent to examine the chart with some pretense of interest. In silence, I spent some minutes studying the convoluted lines that led from Bethlehem to Herb Gillespie in Freeman's Reach.

As we drove away there was a long silence, unusual for him, who filled every second with prattle. Now he was waiting for me to tell him how stunned I was at the revelation. I couldn't help myself. 'What a load of crap,' I said.

'What do you mean! You saw the chart!'

'Anyone could make up a chart like that. You can't possibly take it seriously.'

'Why not? Why shouldn't Herb be descended from Jesus?'

I tried to think of an answer that was theologically irrefutable. I fossicked around among the remnants of my biblical knowledge, gained, but now mostly forgotten, while researching a dismal biblical movie.

'If he was, don't you think he'd be better known?' This was the best I could do. 'He'd be a celebrity if it was genuine, not a farmer in the Hawkesbury valley!'

'He's just modest. He doesn't want people to know.'

I looked across at him. His lower jaw was thrust forward in a way that told me discussion was pointless, as well as tedious.

'You're just a cynic,' he murmured at me, ' you were always like that, even when you were a little boy. You never believe anyone.'

Apart from a football match we went to a couple of weeks later I never saw him alive again. My sister called me in Los Angeles a year later to tell me he'd died while watching cricket on television. I was about to begin a film but delayed it a few days and flew back for the funeral. It was held at a small bush church, miles from the nearest town.

The day was extraordinarily windy, all the eucalypts groaned and rustled. I felt like an extra from an antipodean *Wuthering Heights*. Predictably, there were very few people present. Only my sister and her family and an old couple from the bowling club. Luckily, Herb Gillespie didn't show up, so I was spared any insights his lineage might have provided. A young and absurdly cheerful employee of the funeral director took me to see the body stretched out in an appropriately dimly lit room. 'Big bloke,' he grinned at me, 'I had a lot of trouble squeezing him into that suit.' In fact I'd never seen him look so smart. Suit, white shirt and tie. Alive, he always dressed himself in clothes bought from an opportunity shop which, with their mixture of textures and colours, gave him the air of an old time circus clown.

Two well-dressed elderly couples arrived just before the service. I noticed them and whispered to my sister, but she shook her head. After the brief and unnecessarily perfunctory rites, performed by a bad-tempered minister who was resenting time spent away from golf, or choir boys, I spoke to the late arrivals.

'Were you friends of my father?' I asked, without much interest.

'We're his sisters,' one of them said.

'His sisters?! I didn't know he had any sisters.'

They had seen the death notice we had put in the *Age* and flown up from Melbourne for the funeral of a brother who, I was told, had left home at nineteen, never to return or even contact them again. This was sixty years ago.

'But why would he have done that?'

'We don't know. He was such a nice boy. Very polite and very bright. Mum never got over it.'

My sister and I went through all his papers over the next few weeks, not that there were many of them, thinking we might find some letter relating to his background, his sudden departure from his family. There were a few poems written when he was in his twenties, quite good, I thought, especially coming from someone who had not shown the slightest interest in reading or writing anything. We learnt from the sisters that he had been very disturbed, as a teenager, by the sudden death of another sister, from one of those illnesses that killed in those days but are easily dealt with by an antibiotic today. She had died literally in his arms, we were told.

People are far too complicated and the influences on them too varied for me to think that the sister's death was the 'Rosebud' that explains my father's life, though it must have affected him profoundly. He never mentioned it and people rarely talk about those things that have had the most impact on them.

I still occasionally run into some of his old cronies who invariably say 'Oh, your Dad! What a great bloke he was. So easy-going. Such a lot of fun ...'

CLAIRE HAYWOOD

MEN BEWARE

The search for Mr Right is, for my mother, eternal. It doesn't seem to matter how many Mr Wrongs, Mr Maybes and Mr-Should-Be-Locked Up-And-Throw-Away-The-Keys she has dated in her jam-packed sixty-five years, she has never said die. The fact that a number of her beaux have obliged in this department anyway, has only served to rekindle the flame of romance that burns like an industrial blowtorch in her heart.

Firstly, of course, there was my father. Her one and only true love. 'You never forget the first one, dear,' she litanises regularly. This statement has rather more serious implications than one might think, since my mother suffers, or rather, everyone around my mother suffers while she carries on oblivious, from a short-term memory disability. As a consequence she has not only forgotten the names of all the other men she has either dated or married but she also has a habit of mixing them up. They have, in the end, become one and the same person. Collectively they are Mr Right of the present, past and future — rather like the ghosts of Christmas.

The other relevant detail about my mother is that her memory loss occurred because of a condition which manifested itself when she was thirty-five, and so as a result, like the old grandfather clock in the song, time stopped for her at this precise point. She is and will always be thirty-five and my father will always be Mr Right. The fact that he is not presently *her* Mr Right is purely academic. As far as she is concerned he is still a major presence in her life, despite not having laid eyes on him for over thirty years.

That is, until the day of my wedding when, having at first failed to recognise the man she lived with for fifteen years, she leaned over to me and whispered, her pale blue eyes wide with astonishment:

'What's happened to your father? He looks so *old*?'

'Age does that to people, mother,' I replied drily.

She was not my favourite person at that particular point in time. A report had just gotten back to me that she had accosted my poor uninitiated

The fact that he was two under par at the time only adds to the tragedy. husband-to-be at a delicate moment in the proceedings, namely, minutes before we made our vows, and insisted that he point out the groom to her. When he stammered that he *was* the groom, she declared:

'No, you're not. You're the groom's brother.' This precipitated a fairly instantaneous identity crisis that seemed to last for the entire ceremony and well on into the reception. The fact that he hasn't been quite the same since our wedding day can only be a testament to my mother's ability to send most of her relatives, after five minutes in her company, completely and utterly off the deep end.

But enough of my Mr Right. After my father, who patently left her for another woman but who, by her reckoning, was mysteriously stolen from her, there was the twice-widowed Ron* who had a fondness for alcohol, golf and my mother in that order. I suspected there was something rotten about Ron right from the start. His liver, as it turned out, although mother will never admit it. The scene usually goes as follows:

Daughter: He liked his booze a bit, though.

Mother: (Astonished) Who? Ron? He wasn't a drinker.

Daughter:	Every time I saw him he was tanked to the eyeballs.
Mother:	He liked to have a drink when he went down to the club, that's all.
Daughter:	Starting at nine o'clock in the morning? I'm sorry, mother, but he was permanently paralytic.
Mother:	Well, he was always very nice to me.

At this point I usually take a few beats, wondering whether to remind her of the time he took her to the Sunshine Coast, left her alone in a five star hotel for three days, returning only to lunge at her with a solid silver steak knife in a pathetic attempt to terminate the marriage. I could have asked her how she was able to overpower a six-foot-two ex-airforce captain with her bare hands and lock him in the bathroom while she called room service, but it never seems worth it somehow. Obviously the accommodation made a huge impression, since it is this that takes out first prize in the highly selective memory stakes. Old Ron has simply gone down in her annals of rewritten history as 'a nice chap' whose life ended abruptly on the fourth hole of the

They were in love and love conquers all, including social security fraud.

Brisbane Country Club when he stepped into the path of an oncoming motorised buggy. The fact that he was two under par at the time only adds to the tragedy.

Next there was Walter*. He was a genuinely 'nice chap' who did actually love my mother, but sadly, not as much as he hated himself. *He* wasn't a drinker either. According to mother, Walter was officially 'on the wagon'. Whenever I came to visit, however, he was more often than not, on the flagon; usually of cheap port or brandy, followed by a milk chaser, a cigarette and a large snort of Ventolin from his puffer. Walter was living under an assumed name, or so he confessed to my mother in a moment of self-pitying truth. But when he was found dead on a park bench following a three day absence from their flat, no foul play was suspected. The police didn't bother to find out who he really was and why he was living in a government flat under a false name, and so neither did she. They were in love and love conquers all, including social security fraud.

After Walter, came a string of beaux who should have been strung up. There was Neville* the pill Nazi who would make sure she was well supplied with prescription drugs to keep her suitably sedated, while he wrote himself cheques to cover the cost. Neville tipped himself grandly for this service, before running off with another elderly woman whose mental stability was equally dubious. Mother was adamant that he must have 'put her in the family way'; why else would he have married her so soon after faxing my mother a farewell note? I could have offered a number of reasons, all of them financial, but decided that it was kinder to keep quiet. She continues to this day, whenever she thinks of it, to write letters to Neville, asking him to mail back various personal items of hers, such as her mink coat and her sapphire ring. Needless to say, Neville could give lessons to the great Houdini.

Neville was swiftly replaced by Charlie*, whom she would have married if she hadn't found out he was 'seeing someone else'. This was a moot point since Charlie only had ten percent of his vision. Their courtship ritual consisted of swift walks through dense traffic with Charlie beating out a pathway ahead of them with his white cane. Their song was a cacophony of bleeps and toots and honks and expletives from angry motorists, which fazed mother only slightly and Charlie not at all. He was 'a real gentleman' and his white cane routine made her feel special. Several other ladies shared her feeling and so she left him at the Home For The Blind one bright summer's day with few regrets. Besides, he was a good deal older than her, she being thirty-five, even if he could outwalk her at peak hour.

Charlie's successor was Kevin* the Bereaved, who cried his way into her heart and then, one can only hope, into the little patch of ground he has reserved for himself beside his 'fondly remembered' Amy. Kevin was so suddenly and quite unexpectedly heartbroken over the loss of his wife that he could not bring himself to spend another minute with my mother, having seduced her the night before. Whoever said one night stands were passé in the nineties hasn't been around any retirement villages lately.

After Kevin (or perhaps it was before, since at this point even I can be forgiven for losing track a bit) came Ted*, the army major who checked into my mother's nursing home on a two week respite visit, and checked out in a coffin. Ted was a septuagenarian charmer who made it clear on their first date that there would be no 'hanky-panky'. The war had taken care of him for good in that department, he assured her. But Ted had other, hidden charms. As an army medical officer, he claimed to have worked wonders with hypnotism and one morning after my mother carried his cup of tea to his bedroom, she found herself with her ailing right foot at a ninety degree angle, in close proximity to the aforementioned inactive parts, while he proceeded to hypnotise it. Age shall not weary them indeed! One evening, after a particularly heavy hypnosis session, mother kissed him goodnight and tucked him into his single bed, which was where he was found at noon the next day.

After Ted, my sister and I were convinced that mother was on a roll. The Black Widow of Bondi. It was a grim thought. We tried in vain to persuade her to forego the sexual fast lane in favour of a quiet life of celibacy. She might not live longer but others certainly would. She agreed to lay low for a while, speaking only to strange men on buses and in supermarkets, where they were less likely to be seduced by her gregarious manner and her agreeably dotty, little-girl-lost demeanour, but she was not a happy woman. She still had her eye out for Mr Right. I cited the latest marital statistics and flung facts at her at a furious rate, hoping to convince her that at her age 'the male shortage' was no myth. 'You only have to read the death column to see that women outlive men by far,' I reasoned in desperation. 'There are heaps of women out there who get on perfectly well without a man!' we hinted. 'Just give up, mother!' we pleaded.

But my mother is a true woman of the fifties. She was born with a Hoover in her hand. If she can't clean up after a man, what is there left in

Whoever said one night stands were passé in the nineties hasn't been around any retirement villages lately.

life? At this, my sister and I roll our eyes and bite our tongues in unison. The feminisation of our mother is a Herculean task at which even Germaine Greer in her heyday would have baulked.

When she started making eyes at one of my friends, I realised my mission was doomed to failure.

'But he's my age, mother!' I exclaimed, deeply shocked.

The truth is, I was fighting off the image of my friend in bed beside my ample mother with her eclectic taste in nightwear — a bri-nylon nightie over a thermal wool spencer, topped off by a pair of cotton-tails to protect her tightly-permed Claudette Colbert hairstyle lest it turn into a fright wig the next morning. It was a Fellini-esque vision to rival the master of the grotesque himself.

'Well, how old is that?' she interrupted my nightmare reverie.

'Thirty-five. Ish.'

'Isn't that my age?' She blinked at me, all questioning innocence. There was the hint of a crooked smile on her lips where she'd run off the line with her geranium-red lipstick. I looked at her and decided to let that one pass.

I have tossed in the tea towel when it comes to my mother's quest for domestic bliss. If she wants to go on looking for Mr Right then far be it

from me to cramp
her style. If the best
thing about having
Alzheimer's is that
you can hide your own

The feminisation of our mother is a Herculean task ...

Easter eggs, then the best thing
about my mother's condition is that no
matter how much she has been burned by rela-
tionships in the past, she will persist in beating
her battered wings against the perennial flame of
romance, knowing in her heart of hearts that Mr
Right is still out there somewhere. Who knows?
She might be right. And with all those 'nice
chaps' out there, she's bound to get lucky.

*The names in this story have been changed to protect
the dead.

MARK 'JACKO' JACKSON

KUTA AND THE DEAD BUDGIE EULOGY

What could a group of Mormons in the Arizona desert and the players of the Melbourne Footy Club have in common? Well, besides the obvious — an experience of long droughts — both made me, Mr 'Oi', the Individual, Mark 'Jacko' Jackson, feel like a complete outsider. I believe some French fella, Camoo, wrote whole books about the sort of experience I had. Not that he could have put it any better than Eric Carmen in his classic ditty, 'All By Myself.'

First off, there was the footy trip to Bali with the boys from the Melbourne Footy Club. For those who don't know, that club is known as the Demons, but if they replaced the D with an L, you might get a more appropriate nickname.

Anyway, I was on $12,500 for the year and I'd been fined $13,000, for being late for training, not making the psychiatrist's appointments they had booked for me, and so on. Which meant I had to find my own fare for the end of season trip to Kuta. Maybe they thought I was a bad influence, or maybe they'd snuck a peek at my collection of Boy George records; whatever, I was the only bloke sent to a room by himself.

That first night I could hear all the skylarkin' and carryin' on goin' on round the pool and I sat in me room expectantly awaiting the knock on the door that would herald a night bigger than Demis Roussos' wetsuit. Like Cliff Richard, it never came.

For those who don't know, that club is known as the Demons, but if they replaced the D with an L, you might get a more appropriate nickname.

I guess I was being ostracised. Might I say in my defence though, braggart that I am, I never claimed I had the equipment of anything more than a medium-sized cassowary. Anyway, next morning I got up bright and early and organised orange juice for all my team-mates.

The second night I once again got all dressed up and waited in my room for the friendly invite to frolic in tropical climes. Or at the very least, wash a plateload of magic mushrooms down with some warm Bintang.

By 10.00 p.m. there had still been no knock on the door, the gardenia in my hair was wilting and the old Starsky and Hutch ep I'd been watching was looking good. That's when I knew it was time to get out.

I grabbed a bimo and set sail for a salubrious club called Peanuts. It was about 11.00 when I got there to find the place crawling with gun-toting Malaysians or wherever Bali is part of. Turns out they were the police. There'd been a stabbing there and the joint was shut.

'JACKO IS A WANKEI ASSHOLE', 'JACKO MAKES

My night cruelly circumcised, I hailed another bimo and hit the all night markets at Denpasar. Here I found a bloke with a lot of T-shirts. All night I had been trying to take on board what I had learned about myself; namely, I was about as popular as an award-winning ABC documentary. How could I use this fact to my advantage? I asked the T-shirt merchant if I could buy some blank T-shirts.

'How many?' he asked.

'Ten thousand,' I replied.

'Ten thousand?'

'Yeah, ten thousand.'

He disappeared a moment, then came back with another bloke. We went through the ritual again.

'How many T-shirt you want?'

'Ten thousand'

They took me behind their stall and there sold me ten thousand T-shirts at twenty cents each. I stuffed the whole lot into the bimo and returned to the hotel. Then I transferred them from the bimo to my room.

I'd only just finished when the sun came up. I ordered the bimo back and stuffed the T-shirts back into it. Then I went down to the post office and organised to ship them all back to Melbourne. The next season, outside every ground I played, there were the T-shirts for sale, 'JACKO IS A WANKER', 'JACKO IS AN ASSHOLE', 'JACKO MAKES E.T. LOOK GOOD' and so on ... at twenty dollars a pop.

I never knew it could be so good having so many people hate you.

A few years later I had made my way to Hollywood and thanks to my Energizer ads had landed a role in a TV series, 'The Highwayman'. Before we started shooting, the producer told me, 'Mark — whatever you do, don't tell Sam Jones you're getting more than him.'

Sam Jones was the star. I guess that was because he owns more turkeys than the Ingham Brothers.

We were shooting in Arizona, it was 39 degrees

in the shade and the nearest shade was in Michigan. There was nothing but cacti and Mormons. The whole crew were Mormons. During night shoots they'd sit around the campfire and sing Osmonds' favourites.

Anyway, I think I got off on the wrong foot with everyone when the pet budgie of the make-up Mormon mysteriously died.

The third assistant Mormon came around to my trailer with a card to sign — you know, like they do when you fall off the perch. The others were very eloquent in their praise of the budgie; JFK and Martin Luther King would have been envious. I would have been eloquent too, but it was too hot and I was in this leather outfit. So I just wrote, 'Sorry about the budgie'.

That's what started it. I think even the gaffer Mormons expected something more poetic.

Things got worse when Sam, our star, kept coming on set late. I put up with it for a while, then I had a word to him. It worked for about a week. Then this particular day he was late three times in a row.

My make-up was running, the leather was melting — I was like an old 45 left on the back shelf of the Ford Futura on a summer's day. I was warping! I blew my stack at Sam, I called him a f&*^%^ing this and a f%$@*^&ing that.

He went right off at me. He explained how he was the 'star' and how he was not to be spoken to in such a manner. When he lunged at me, I grabbed him and pulled him to my buckles.

I'm the only joker who knows the words to all those Osmonds' tunes.

The sun had been on them for forty-five minutes and I swear you could hear his ears sizzle as they came in contact with the gleaming chrome. Something cut him too.

Sam stomped off to his trailer with a bloodied cheek and then the rest of the crew turned on me and hissed 'Blasfemur'. I wasn't sure what one of those was but I knew it wasn't good. Horses have femurs so I could only guess that what they were saying was a Mormon thing that meant 'horse's arse' but in a nice way.

Back in my trailer the phone rang. It was the head of NBC. He told me I should pull my head in if I wanted the show to continue.

I'd been carpeted by Barassi and Hafey so this wasn't too hard to handle.

Next the producer rang. He told me that I'd offended the director, the star and the cameraman. He patiently explained that it was the star's prerogative to make everybody else wait on them.

Basically, in Hollywood you got paid to be treated like shit until such a time when you came to be the star and could treat everybody else like shit.

Again, a bit like a footy coach.

I saw the light and apologised for my tirade.

'That's okay,' he said, 'so long as you didn't tell Sam you were getting more than him?'

'No, I never went that far'

'That's okay then, mate'.

Sadly, 'The Highwayman' only went the one series. If it had gone another, I might have been a millionaire.

Still, the exercise wasn't a total waste. I am the only person who can prove he stopped a big semi with his magic boomerang. I've got the footage.

And I get free entry into every retro disco night in THE WORLD cause I'm the only joker who knows the words to all those Osmonds' tunes.

Lex Marinos

SCIENCE IS A HEALTH HAZARD

At the risk of offending you by stating the obvious, but for the benefit of those who may be from another planet, we may as well all start from the basic irrefutable premise that science was invented by the Greeks. To prove that it is indeed a health hazard, I need do no more than rattle a few skeletons from within my own family's closet. Let's take the case of the unfortunate Archimedes. Or to give him his full name, Archimedes Marinopoulos. This is the man that science would have you believe discovered that a body displaces its own weight when submerged in water. He allegedly discovered this when he plunged into a full bath after a hard day's physics, and was surprised when the water overflowed, soaking through the lino and dripping

A childhood encounter with a Gorgon had left him a little simple, or one side short of a square as we used to say.

onto the tenants in the flat below. Then, allegedly, he ran naked down the street proclaiming 'Eureka, eureka!' which was ancient Greek for 'I've found it, I've found it!' The truth as handed down from generation to generation in my family is this: Archimedes was indeed naked and more to the point, he was naked for the first time in his life. He was always accustomed to bathing in his clothes as a way of saving on laundry expenses. Consequently, he did run around yelling that he had found it, but what exactly he was so delighted to have found, family honour forbids me from elaborating upon.

As for displacing his own weight in water, once again the facts have been grossly distorted over the millennia. The truth? Well, one day he was coming back from Delphi, where he had been consulting the oracle, trying to gain some early clues on how to split the atom, and he missed the last ferry which crossed the Gulf of Corinth to our village of Rizomilos. He was going to swim when he reasoned that he would get there quicker if he was the same weight as the ferry. He then proceeded to bundle statues and temple ruins into his tunic and dived in. We like to think that he died happily having discovered that the heavier you are, the quicker you drown.

Then there was the unfortunate Pythagoras, or to give him his full name, Pythagoras Karofilis. He was from my mother's side of the family. A childhood encounter with a Gorgon had left him a little simple, or one side short of a square as we used to say. And indeed it was his fascination with three-sided shapes that led him to discover the equilateral triangle, the isosceles triangle, and the love triangle. It was this last one that killed him. Being exactly five feet tall, imagine his delight when he discovered a pair of Syracusan sisters th at were exactly four feet and three feet tall respectively. Having successfully wooed them, he finally persuaded them to lie down with him. He carefully placed them at right angles to one another, and just as he was about to square his hypotenuse, their father who was precisely six foot five burst in, bisected Pythagoras and then dissected him. The last triangle Pythagoras ever saw was in Bermuda.

Sad to say, later generations of scientists ignored the calamities of my antecedents, to their own peril. Let's take the case of Isaac Newton. As a young man, Newton showed great promise as a maths teacher, until one day, during recess, he happened to be hit a fearful blow on the head by an apple. During the ensuing coma, he formulated his theory of gravitation, namely that 'there is a force of attraction between any two massive particles in the universe' and can be expressed thus: $F=m1m2G/d^2$. This formula is engraved in the minds of sky divers so they can measure the amount of fun they are having, where F is for fun =man1xman2xGranny Smith (which features in all of Newton's theories thereafter) divided by death to the power of two. Newton also played around with the laws of motion, the third one of which was that for every action there is an equal and opposite reaction. In other words, x=y, which from that point on led Newton to call a box a boy, sox were soy, and no doubt he would have called Mad Max, Mad May.

Around about the same time as Newton was being treated for concussion, the Irish physicist Robert Boyle was formulating his law, which is that 'the volume of a given mass of gas at a constant temperature is inversely proportional to its pressure' (pV=constant). And how did Boyle discover this? Well, he was a director of the East India Company, and on one of his excursions into the Punjab he consumed a particularly spicy curry, which, combined with the climate on the subcontinent caused him a great deal of heat stress. The only way he could gain any relief was to go home and sit in the fridge. As he sat there in the dark, the light being off because he had to have the door closed so the temperature would remain constant, eventually he noticed his stomach was distended due to the accumulation of gas from the curry. Being a gentleman, of course, he didn't want to fart in the fridge, and the only relief he could obtain was from pushing his stomach back in. The harder he pushed, the smaller the volume of gas became. This led him to discover that pork vindaloo remains constant. This episode impaired his health to such an extent that the only notable achievement in his subsequent career was the failure to perfect the matchstick.

The twentieth century has been dominated by two scientists; both in their own way were basket cases. The first, Albert Einstein, made three revolutionary discoveries, and here you will really have to pay attention. Firstly, that time is the fourth dimension; secondly, that everything can be converted into something else and become interchangeable; and thirdly, truth is not absolute but relative to the circumstances of the person measuring it and dependent on the type of drugs you are taking. Einstein concluded that basically the mass of something is a measure of its energy content, and could be formulated thus: $E=mc^2$. Now while this is a good working formula for nearly everything, it also serves as a very personal description of Einstein himself, whereby Einstein equals meat times carbohydrate squared, or to put it another way, one all-beef patty on a sesame seed bun. That's right, Albert Einstein is Ronald MacDonald.

The other great scientific genius of our times

was, of course, Julius Sumner Miller. He was the man who discovered how to put a hard-boiled egg into a milk bottle. Eating the egg now becomes a huge scientific challenge, not to mention getting your toasted Vegemite fingers in and out of the bottle. Julius found that the most effective way of eating the egg was to put a whole lot more burning paper into the bottle, sit on top of it and wait to be sucked inside the bottle yourself. The hazards to one's health become obvious. If you want to live a healthy, productive life, avoid science at all costs.

$$E=mc^2$$

DENNIS ALTMAN

CONGRESS

The Feminist Novelist was not amused.

Deirdre and I had come in from dinner, giggling together in delighted complicity. 'Marilyn,' said Deirdre, 'let me tell you a story.'

Deirdre had, as is the custom of literary events, been conducting an affair with an exiled Iranian poet, referred to, in homage to both his literary skills and his personal stubbornness, as the Celestial.

Having seen Deirdre leave last night's dinner with me, the Celestial had thrown a fit of jealousy, despite her attempts to reassure him.

'Don't be stupid,' she'd protested, 'he's a homosexual. Gay.' The word meant nothing to Abou, nor was it to be found in the pocket Persian-English phrase book they had used to bridge earlier misunderstandings. One gathered they had retired to separate bedrooms, and that the Celestial was still brooding.

'How could you,' expostulated the Feminist Novelist. 'How could you have anything to do with a man who behaves as if he owns you?' For Marilyn, this was clearly nothing to laugh about.

In her defence it must be said that humour was not in much evidence at the Thirty-Sixth Annual Congress of the World Assembly of Literature (or, as Angus Wilson might have put it, *The Old Men at the Zoo*).

No expense had been spared to bring us together in immoderate comfort: poets from Peru, novelists from Norway, translators from Tunisia had been jetted across the world, sometimes with spouse or companion — business class if they were particularly favoured by the organisers — and dumped in the lobby of the Grand Ritz Harbourside, with its two revolving restaurants, its three piano bars and enough ice to douse the Nullarbor.

Nobel Prize winners, Pulitzer Prize winners, novelists whose books are regularly reviewed on the front page of the *New York Times* and the *TLS*, playwrights whose plays were the talk of last year's season in Wellington and Sofiya, and a surprising number of apparently penniless poets flowed through the lobbies, one eye constantly on the alert — 'Have you seen Soyinka? Nadine?

Prahbwala?' — while literary journalists, most of them freelance and willing to quote anyone for a free drink, cornered ageing national treasures and sought their views on the Canadian situation while trying to figure out who they were.

'I can't find Anthony,' said Deirdre, speaking of her fellow Australian delegate.

I went in search to the bar. A young Dutch poet, lank from too many gins, smiled at my WAL badge.

'Sit,' he said expansively, waving at the row of empty stools beside him.

'I'm looking for an Australian writer,' I said. 'Anthony McGuin.'

The poet leant back and peered into the face of a youngish woman who was sitting at a small barside table, reading the *Globe and Mail*.

'Are you Australian?' he asked, his eyes boring through her paper.

She looked startled. 'I'm with the Young Homemakers of America,' she said finally.

'Doesn't matter,' said Hans, leering. 'You could be Australian if you wanted to.' He waved me away, and turned back to the Young Homemaker. 'Have a drink,' he said.

'I don't think he's here,' said Deirdre. 'You'll have to be the other delegate.'

But I'm not even a member of WAL. I just happened to be in Toronto.'

'So? You're Australian and you write and I'm

not going to the Assembly of Delegates on my own.'

Deirdre pinned an outsize badge on my sweater, proclaiming me a delegate. 'You're credentialled now,' she said, tugging me into the McKenzie King-Wilfrid Laurier Memorial Ballroom.

The delegates sat in long serried rows facing a top table at which various eminences of the World Assembly of Literature were slumped, looking rather like a group of men waiting for admission to a nursing home. One woman sat among them, but she, as the very severity of her hair suggested, was there to take the minutes.

'So what do we do?' I hissed at Deirdre, who was looking round vaguely, hoping for inspiration.

She shrugged. 'Count the hours until lunchtime I guess.'

The President shuffled onto the stage, a cadaverous man in a funeral suit who had, it was rumoured, been a coming figure in Paris between the wars, and had once given a recipe to Alice B Toklas. We had already heard him speak the night before, a long paean to literature, the French language, the importance of the novel and the Canadian landscape, all of which he described in long flowery sentences which left his translators gasping for breath and his audience restless.

Today, however, it was not he but the Secretary-General who was to dominate. A Pole by birth, who had lived in Germany, Switzerland and France, and spoke all their languages perfectly, even, it was said, Romansh, he sat back in his chair with an air of careless imperiousness, puffing reflectively on a long cigarette holder, and occasionally waving — no, signalling with his hand — as some particularly favoured delegate took his, less often her, seat.

'Si je me permets, Monsieur Le Président,' he whispered audibly to the President, 'on peut commencer dans quelques minutes.'

'Ah oui,' said Monsieur Le Président decisively. 'Bien sûr.'

Then followed a steady progression through reports, statements of support and financial details which even I, hardened by academic meetings, found insufferably boring. Late in the morning, however, just when I was wondering whether to fake a stomach ache and make for the pool, there came an issue, and one where Deirdre and I could Adopt A Position. Take A Stand. Even, perhaps, Strike A Blow For Freedom.

The next international gathering of the World Assembly was scheduled for Cartagena, Colombia, a city described in the glossy brochures we had been handed as: 'One of the most picturesque cities in Latin America, noted for its plazas and narrow cobblestoned streets, its memories of the days when buccaneers roamed the Spanish Main.' Unfortunately, as the brochure went on to tell us, the city government planned the World Assembly as the centrepiece of its celebrations of the five hundredth anniversary of Colombus' discovery of the Americas, to which certain indigenous groups had taken exception.

Passionate speeches about the role of writers thus followed, with appropriate denunciations of imperialism, colonialism and exploitation, usually delivered by delegates from rich countries who could, no doubt, experience a warm frisson of self-righteousness by retrospectively condemning the exploits of the Spanish court in the sixteenth century. The South American delegates were less convinced, particularly when the alternative sites proposed — Bratislava or Lyon — meant that the first ever meeting of the World Assembly in the South would once again be postponed.

'How can it be the South?' expostulated one of the many vice-chairmen from the stage, who had the benefit of a British degree in geography. 'Colombia is north of the equator.'

'South meaning the dispossessed,' replied a Brazilian delegate angrily. 'All those of us who come from the countries you like to refer to as underdeveloped. Whose hospitality you would scorn.'

'I don't know,' said Deirdre anxiously. 'We lose

either way. If we vote for Colombia we vote for Cortés, Pizarro and the extermination of the Indians. If we vote against, we vote for retaining the dominance of the Atlantic North against the struggling South.'

'I think we should support the boycott of the First Peoples,' I insisted. 'It's the same issue as our Bicentennial and the Aborigines.'

'Right,' said Deirdre. 'Get up and say so.'

I made a short intervention to the effect that while we would very much like to meet in Latin America (I have personally always wanted to see Rio) we felt it would be unfortunate to link the World Assembly too closely to any government-run and controversial commemoration. 'After all,' I concluded, 'our only justification is that we remain independent of all governments, and speak the truth as we see it.'

This piece of premodernist rhetoric went down well, particularly with delegates from those countries which still believe in 'the truth', and possess Ministries of Culture to promote it.

Not all the speeches, of course, posed the question so directly; writers are used to metaphor, to symbolism, and thus the delegate from Estonia (resident in Topeka, Kansas) spoke for fifteen minutes on the suppression of the Estonian culture after the Hitler-Stalin pact, and the delegate from Puerto Rico explained at great length that any plebiscite in which his people voted to retain links with the United States would be a clear act of cultural genocide. The Feminist Novelist leapt to the microphone to point out it would also be gynocide, and asked why there were no people of colour, no disabled and only one woman on the stage. After several more such speeches, including a denial by the Korean delegate that his government ever had or ever would discriminate against anyone for any reasons, the Secretary-General leant forward.

'**H**onestly,' hisse Deirdre, 'if he were woman I'd accuse you of sexual harassment.'

'Si je me permets, Monsieur Le Président ...' he sibilated, 'et si mes amis colombiens sont d'accord,' with a nod towards them, 'I propose we refer the matter to our executive committee, which can fully reflect on the important issues raised this morning by so many distinguished delegates.'

'Au oui,' said Monsieur Le Président. 'Bien sûr. In any case,' (I translate loosely here) 'there is no question of Colombia. There are bandits. Drug kings. Whereas in Lyon ...'

A tactful cough from the Secretary-General, as he leant across and, I suspect — but have no proof — adjusted the volume of the President's microphone. 'It is almost lunchtime. Maybe we could adopt the motion to refer the matter elsewhere ...?

'Ah oui,' said the President decisively. 'I so adopt.' He rose. 'A table,' he said.

As we started to leave the hall, a young woman from Canada expostulating behind us, the Secretary-General came up to me. 'Yes, a very interesting point of view,' he said, taking me by the arm. 'Unfortunately the demands of the budget do not always allow us such, shall I say, purity of motive. But perhaps you would like to assist us in this problem? There is room for several panels at Cartagena, and if you were to participate it would guarantee that your point of view is expressed ...'

'But you're assuming we shall meet at Cartagena?'

'No, no,' protested the Secretary-General, 'it is not I who can decide such matters. It is only that experience suggests, may I be so bold, that when we have already commenced our planning it is always difficult to reverse ... And, of course, we shall be able to discuss the issue so much more fully if the topic is listed on the program.' His grip on my arm tightened imperceptibly. 'I am sure,' he said, 'that you would enjoy visiting Colombia, and should there be a problem with funds, our travel budget, while not overgenerous, does provide for panel members ...'

That evening, the third gala of the Congress, found tempers a little frayed. One of the American delegates had fled back to New York, after, it was rumoured, one of his colleagues had thrown herself at his feet and proclaimed undying passion. Two writers from Sri Lanka had come down with food poisoning after sampling local cuisine, and a Filipina, who had never been seen without several inches of make-up and Paris-label clothes, had wandered off and not been seen since the previous night. We finally discovered Anthony McGuin, who had been delayed after changing planes twice en route, both times finding himself unexpectedly in Dallas.

Hordes of locals, attracted by the literary glamour and free booze, circulated through the cavernous hall of Toronto's Art Centre, while I made desultory attempts to chat up passing waiters. One in particular, a willowy blond whose name-tag proclaimed him to be called Tigger, caught my eye. 'Honestly,' hissed Deirdre, 'if he were a woman I'd accuse you of sexual harassment.'

'He enjoys the attention. Don't you?'

Tigger grinned. 'I collect admirers,' he said. 'Have another canapé.'

As the crowds began thinning I noticed that the Secretary-General was preparing to leave the event in the company of a tall woman, dressed in

Deirdre's friend. The homosexual.'
He took me aside. 'I didn't fully
comprehend last time we met. I was
foolishly jealous.'

black
chiffon, whose stance
seemed familiar, if not as familiar as
the Secretary-General's arm, which was draped
proprietarily around her shoulder. At the door
they turned, and he squeezed her closer to him. It
was the Feminist Novelist.

'Ah well,' said Deirdre, 'at least she should get
a trip to Cartagena out of him. Like the rest of
you.'

I protested my innocence, while mentally
working out itineraries: one would have to
connect in Mexico City, I thought, or maybe take
the new transpolar flight to Buenos Aires.

As it happened the next meeting of the World
Assembly was moved from Cartagena after presi-
dential drug summits pre-empted writers as
attractions in the eyes of the City Council. The
President of the World Assembly managed to
schedule the conference for Lyon as a parting
gesture before being finally incommoded by a
stroke. I went to Lyon, but on my own money,
although I doubt as much of the Feminist
Novelist and the Celestial.

The Celestial's English had considerably

improved, I was pleased to note. 'Ah,' he said, greeting me with some warmth. 'Deirdre's friend. The homosexual.' He took me aside. 'I didn't fully comprehend last time we met. I was foolishly jealous. This time,' he said pressing my hand, 'I am sure we can be friends.'

Which seems an appropriately ambivalent point at which to end this story. For it is, after all, fiction, despite its apparent similarity to another congress of another writers' organisation of which I wrote an account in the weekend press. None of these characters exist, although each had her or his simulacrum in real life. Whether what happened in a mythical conference in the future in Lyon is more accurate than what happened in a real conference last October in Toronto is for you to decide. A hackneyed point perhaps, but at least post-modern literary theory provides writers with new devices to exit from unfinished stories.

ROB SITCH

BENCHMARK

This Christmas, as you sit down to open the presents, benchmark your family. My family has done it for years. I was reminded of it by the recent McKinsey study that compares the productivity of various Australian industries against the best in the world. Apparently no gold medals for us there. I'm not sure whether any Australian industries were spraying champagne on the victory dais, but it served to underline how important the concept of benchmarking is.

It rests on the inalienable concept that everything can be measured in dollar terms. Here's an idea of how our family benchmarking goes. One year my brother hand-made a beautiful wooden frame and in it had a blown-up photograph of Mum's new grandson. I gave Mum a fifty dollar note — wrapped, of course.

An independent assessor valued my brother's present at $46 and so, using my present as a benchmark of one hundred, my brother's over-capitalised gift came in at only ninety-two. I was roughly 1.1 times a better son than he. The multiple has been as high as two. That was another time he stupidly went for one of those handmade things with little salvageable value. I gave money again. (I had to remind Mum of that as she spent most of the day gazing at the photo and virtually ignoring the cash.)

It's important to benchmark everything. For most of that year, he was a 1.5 times better conversationalist at the dinner table. We had databases on everything because, well, you know, those rules again: everything can be measured and everything should be improved. We must never be content. So when you sit down for the family festivities, run the mental callipers over your family. Measure them, compare them, equate it to a base and tell them whether they are good or bad. Otherwise you may fall for the silly trap of assessing things on an emotional level.

Now I've got nothing against the McKinsey study per se, it's just that I'm suspicious of purely economic measurements. Growing up, we were beaten around the head with how well Singapore was doing and how much more like Singapore we should be. Now I fell for this too ... then I went there. It was the most sterile, charmless, uniform place I had ever been. It was totally 'benchmarked'. It was like a living embodiment of all the wishes of whingeing talkback callers. Short hair, shirts tucked in, clean, with roving bands of enforcement officers spot-fining anything that moved — and absolutely nothing happening! I found one interesting place: the old town. Our hosts proudly told us how quickly it was being torn down.

But, by crikey, did they have an efficient port! You should have seen it. I benchmarked it on the back of an envelope and gave it ninety-seven on a bad day.

The whole experience made me understand what an autocratic pain in the arse Lee Kuan Yew must have been. That real headmaster type that has been something of a role model in Asia. Now he was a benchmarker, a top-notch benchmarker. Ratings of personal freedom weren't included of course: well, they couldn't be, not when you've got a port like that.

I had to laugh recently. An economist in the US came up with a new benchmarking system called Total Factor Productivity, which basically said that when you look

So when you sit down for the family festivities, run the mental callipers over your family.

at all the capital Singapore has employed, it has been going backwards for about a decade. Do you think the benchmarkers took that well? Lee gave him a detention and his parents have been informed.

Now I've got nothing against a good port system, and having laboured under one that stinks for three decades, it would make a nice change. But since not even Keating has been able to force much reform, that particular benchmark is headed south. As for the others: well, productivity is great and laudable but it doesn't seem to capture everything. Maybe having 30% too many bank branches is one of the really pleasant things about this country. It's probably not, but you never know ...

So, as we sit down to enjoy the festive season yet again, let's all have a 1.3 times merrier Christmas and a 14% happier New Year.

STEPHEN MUECKE

URBAN POSTMODERN TRIBES

We saw a re-enactment of a flogging at Old
Sydney Town. Can you believe this? The convict
was Andrew, who usually works at The
Bookshop in Darlinghurst. We *had* snorted a
couple of lines behind the koala sanctuary and
would have broken up completely except for one
thing. Andrew was actually crying, so we didn't
want to spoil it for him.

At the P & C meeting, the Aboriginal guest spoke
in favour of a more liberal attitude towards kids
who spoke Aboriginal English. All the audience
already had this attitude and listened politely to
his anecdotes of discrimination. Only the

Aborigino-crat from the Education Department attacked him on an obscure funding issue.

Meanwhile, next-door in the gym the Tae Kwon Do class, full of middle-aged men, practised to a recording of didgeridoo music.

Jay met Sabrina at Simon Andrew's Saloon Bar on Parramatta Road — pure hyper-real Western. Linda Hutcheon was singing C & W in a light blue chamois cowgirl outfit that would break your heart.

When Georgio arrived carrying a press camera the management was quick to point out that photographs weren't allowed. Some joint in Tasmania was trying to steal the design concept.

Mary-Anne is in Art Direction and lives in Port Melbourne in a town house which is all matt black and halogens. With the recession she has had to trade in her Merc on something 'less aggressive'.

'Anyway, Jojo said that if I ever got a Roller he'd kick the door in.'

'You've really got to get out of the city every other weekend, to 'oxygenate'. I tell you what, in five years time Justine and I will have set up our own company in Byron Bay, she with her fashion, and me with my art things and management skills.'

My film on dental dams is going really well. A lot of the women have come to revalorise the confessional mode of discourse and see themselves as engaged in a self-help community care project.

JACQUI LANG

PSST!

I rely on my humble plastic phone to feed me a melange of slimy, sexy, soiled secrets. Thankfully, it always delivers, a stream of voices offering spicy scraps of scandal which keep me employed.

'Can you believe it? When he's not on TV, he beats up drag queens!' hisses one.

'She got to her dressing-room to find her personal assistant making love to her boyfriend!' laughs another.

I work as a gossip columnist. If TV stars are having threesomes, the voices — some from friends, some from strangers — like to let me know. 'Juicy, but I can't print it,' I often sigh — though I've enjoyed hearing about it anyway.

'That athlete and his 'fairytale wedding' you wrote about last week — I saw him sneaking out of a hotel with his ex a couple of days ago,' a rasping stranger will volunteer.

'Interesting, but we can't write it,' I must reply. *And he looked so reformed at the wedding.*

If only defamation laws didn't exist! They prevent me sharing the tale of the TV reporter sprung — and filmed — having a quickie 'on the job'; Mickey Rooney's story of the happily married Hollywood sex symbol who really prefers pretty lads; of how lovestruck Australian females vied to get physical in the dressing-room with Magic Johnson, despite his HIV status. Too often, one can only hint, not print ...

The challenge of the job is finding titillating tidbits which can be reported.

I try!

My love for spreading gossip began over a bubbling vat of fat fifteen years ago. I was a teenager, fresh out of a proper Presbyterian girls school and I landed a job on Rottnest Island, selling fish and chips at the Rotto Tearooms. Outside, daily, seagulls would squawk and squabble for scraps. And they weren't the only ones displaying their ugly side. Drunken humans would often do the same. And then there were my co-workers; drifters mostly, who lived by their own set of rules.

There was a lean, hunched individual called Ewan. He used to frown a lot as he carved meat into slices all day long. Ewan was a killer.

For the next few hundred hamburger orders, I waited on tenterhooks for a juicy update to the love triangle. Would it culminate in a murder?

Yes, somewhere in his murky, pre-Rollo Take away past, Ewan had killed another. 'It *was* self-defence,' he told me solemnly, eyes aglitter, waving the meat cleaver to make his point, once I'd summoned the nerve to ask him about the rumours. Surprisingly, he'd been more than keen to blab about his felony.

'It was a fight. The other guy was trying to get me. He had to go.' Er, quite.

Ewan's favourite friend at work was Karen, a beefy, brusque blonde who also worked in the kitchen. But one day I came to work to find Ewan wasn't around — he had badly cut his hand. It was Australia Day, the busiest day of the year at Rottnest.

'How did Ewan hurt himself?' I asked Karen, as hordes of drunken day-trippers invaded the shop, demanding fags and hamburgers.

She looked at me with distaste and waddled off to serve someone. 'Haven't you heard?' Mike, another worker, hissed above the din. 'He punched his hand against the wall when he found out Karen had been rooting Percy.'

Percy was a shifty, weatherbeaten local with a

wrinkly prune-like head, who smoked bongs from dawn to dusk. He lived fifty metres away from the Tearooms, next to the Quokka Arms, and loved boasting that his two-year-old lad was learning how to smoke bongs too.

'So why did Ewan punch the wall?' I asked, after digesting the concept of Percy intertwined with rotund Karen.

'Don't you know anything? Karen's been shagging Ewan for weeks — she cheated on him!' Mike sighed at my ignorance.

Aha. I caught on, finally. Somehow Karen had decided that Percy — whose wife was nine months pregnant — was a sexy alternative to Ewan. Karen had clearly believed it was worth the risk to cheat on her killer boyfriend by sneaking off at night on her bike to hook up with sleazy Percy. Who was to say Ewan wouldn't decide they too, had 'to go'? For the next few hundred hamburger orders, I waited on tenterhooks for a juicy update to the love triangle. Would it culminate in a murder?

It didn't — but one day I arrived at work to learn that Karen had abruptly left the island. This was so much better than 'Number 96'! And quite a contrast to life at PLC.

Then there was Andrew the milkshake maker, who also worked at the takeaway section; a silent, surly type who always wore the same daggy pleated navy slacks. As he worked, his long silver necklace would swing in and out of the drinks he was preparing.

'What is on the end of that chain, Andrew?' I asked him one day.

'My girlfriend's teeth,' he replied.

'Pardon?'

'She died in a car accident. I was there. So I kept the teeth.'

As you do. Those rotting fangs must have added a unique flavour to some of those spearmint milkshakes.

My girlfriends would ring me up to see how I was enjoying the job. 'Great,' I'd say. 'But let me tell you about these people I'm working with ...'

A Penthouse Pet has sex with Kevin Costner, then tells me all about it. ('On a scale of one to ten, he was 100!')

And it was then that I realised I enjoyed sharing stories about people doing odd things. It was worth being nosey and asking them awkward questions. Because, more often than not, they'd happily regale you with answers. Eg: Yes, I'm rooting Percy. Yes, I killed someone. Yes, they are my dead girlfriend's fangs.

In all, I worked at Rottnest for two fascinating months. The next challenge was to find a job where one could make use of all the chit-chat, tit-tat. Yes, journalism was the answer!

Fast-forward fifteen years. Now I work on magazines in Sydney, where we can observe Michael Hutchence and Paula Yates in trouble again. Movie stars sneak in and out having affairs with local starlets and liaisons with hookers. A *Penthouse* Pet has sex with Kevin Costner, then tells me all about it. ('On a scale of one to ten, he was 100!') Ditto, a dancer who 'did' Sting ('We made love with my shoes on all night — he was fantastic'), and two women who whipped their gear off in a private sex show for Tom Jones ('His physique is unreal — for a guy his age he's just beautiful.')

But nothing shocks me. Nothing is even weird or wacky — they're all just variations on the theme of sex, betrayal, and death. I've seen it all at Rotto. It's the best training a gossip columnist could ever have had.

PAUL DEMPSEY

THE HEAT IS ON IN SAIGON

I arrived at the Saigon Hotel, a relic from the 1960s, to find Curt in the restaurant with the laptop and printer already set up. Such dedication! 7.30 am on a Monday. Like many of the Vietnam foreign legion, Curt runs a sideline business in addition to whatever it is he overcharges his multinational employer for. Curt's sideline is printing business cards. He prints a lot of cards, but then he needs to. He drinks a lot of gin and tonics, and it's better they don't appear on the monthly expense chit he faxes head-office in Paris.

'What name today?' Curt asked.

'Rodney Cuthbertson QCI. Very English don't you reckon?'

Curt's smile was broader than that jewelled belt Elvis used to wear during his flares phase. I explained to Curt that QCI stood for Quality Control Inspector. Getting into the spirit of things, Curt made up some appropriately toffee sounding, English address and set the printer in motion.

As the set of six business cards rolled off the bubble-jet printer, Rocket appeared, looking very much as one does after twenty-five beers and a ten hour flight from Aus. My mate Rocket was the fastest rover from the Riverina who never played for the Swans, and even though he'd slowed down in the last fifteen years, the name Rocket had stuck.

'Rocket, mate, you look like shit. Here, have one of these.'

The local coffee has more kick than Tony Lockett's right boot — it will either fix you up or kill you, but by the look of Rocket, either way would be an improvement. I had a mission, and I needed Rocket's help, but I felt it was better he didn't quite yet know what was required of him.

Curt handed over the cards to the bemused Rocket and said, 'I hope you like them, good luck. I gotta go.' Then he put his mobile office over his shoulder and disappeared into the mass of French tourists streaming into the restaurant for the free breakfast which would keep them going during their day tour in an old, Russian-made bus, crammed to overflowing.

The dilapidated city is now called Ho Chi

Minh City, but to tourists from France it is still their colony, and let nobody tell them otherwise.

Rocket took his bleary eyes from the Gallic feeding frenzy and said, 'What's this about business cards? I'm here for a holiday'.

As a friend of fifteen years, I felt I owed the Rocket some explanation — if not yet the entire one.

'Look, I know this is your first day but I'm busy as hell. Tag along with me, it'll be fun and it's the best way to see the town. Not like those pigs at the troughs. They only get to see old churches and markets that sell original antique copies.'

The images from US film and television form a huge cultural Camelot for the Vietnamese and Mac had modelled himself on Donahue.

A little confused, Rod persisted with, 'What's with these business cards and what is a QCI?'

'I'll explain in the car. We've got an important meeting in Song Be Province at ten and it's a fair drive, so finish your coffee and let's hit the frog and toad.'

Leaving the Saigon Hotel in Dong Du Street is harder than a Linda Lovelace co-star. Beggars, hawkers and shoe-shine kids zero in on every foreigner that dares leave the sanctuary of the lobby. Fair dinkum, Ripley had an easier time with the aliens. Even though I had lived in the same hotel for three years now, the beggars harassed me with the same zeal as if I had just arrived. Rodney had, of course, only arrived late the night before and now as we walked from the air-conditioned comfort of the Saigon Hotel to the searing, humid heat, he got his first real taste of Ho Chi Minh street life. 'Piss off, ya little shit,' was his first salvo for Aust-Nam relations as he pushed through the wedge of shoe-shine kids offering a quick clean in exchange for a greenback.

Opening the door of the old Mercedes was my driver, Mac. He liked the name Mac because he thought it sounded very American. With the pending lifting of the US Trade Embargo, most Vietnamese were expecting their lot to change overnight. They couldn't wait for drive-ins, woodies and shopping trolleys. Mac was no different. The images from US film and television form a huge cultural Camelot for the Vietnamese and Mac had modelled himself on Donahue — not the talk-show host but Troy. Saigon had not yet abandoned the sixties. *A Summer Place* was still playing somewhere in an underground cinema and Annette Funicello was still considered the height of erotic entertainment.

Even though it was early in the morning and the car was a hop-skip from the hotel, it was enough to work up a sweat. Fortunately, the thoughtful Mac had the air-con already up full.

'So mate, what's with these business cards?' Rocket lets out before we are one block into our journey.

I felt it was time to explain my predicament. I had contracted several hundred thousand pairs of sports shoes for a German client and production had fallen behind by almost eight weeks. I was in deep shit. The factory had accepted every order they had received over the last six months, even though they had no chance of filling them all. Their solution was to produce small quantities of each order, hoping that would keep everybody appeased. This sort of tactic spelled big trouble for yours truly. I had a penalty clause in my contract with the Germans. Failure to deliver on time would see me up for 2 USD per shoe — enough to send me back to Aus with not even a tail to put between my legs. Today's trip to the factory was one last throw of the dice. I had to convince the manager to complete my contract.

Rocket's tactic would have been as effective as a push-up bra on Jeannie Little.

'Sue the bastard if he can't make the shoes on time.'

I would have hated to cross paths with Rocket if he was ever on a bench other than a footy team's.

'Impossible.'

Despair was leaking from me the way moisture was spitting out of the Merc's air-con.

'Maybe I can be the buyer from Germany? I'll tell this bloke if he doesn't finish my contract on time, I'll never place another order.'

Rocket was being very supportive but unfortunately the current attitude of the factories was to make hay while the sun shone. Only a few years before, factories such as the one where we were headed, were lying idle. Now, with the doors of trade open a crack, businessmen such as myself had shouldered in. What we were discovering was that the people with whom we were dealing had little idea how business operated in the free market. To them, the few of us who had already set up shop, seemed like an avalanche. Rocket's tactic would have been as effective as a push-up bra on Jeannie Little. The factory manager already imagined a multitude of foreign businessmen waiting to crawl over broken glass from Hamburg to Ho Chi Minh.

I'll do all the talking. You just agree.

No, a simple threat of no future business was by no means creative or sneaky enough to get me off the hook.

Our first stop was a small cafe ten minutes from the Saigon Hotel where we we picked up

Mr Duc, manager of my shoe business. With him Mr Duc had the only colour chart in existence in Vietnam. These colour charts showed hundreds of variations of every colour. Duc was just as worried as me at the prospect of the meeting. If I failed, he lost his job.

After Rocket had been introduced as Mr Rodney Cuthbertson, Duc enquired as to strategy.

'Well, Mr Duc, I am still formulating that, although I have an idea.'

Rocket eyed me suspiciously.

'I thought I might cancel that other order for 60,000 men's leather shoes.'

Mr Duc looked at me as though I'd suggested making Hush-puppies out of the skins of little children.

'You can't. There's nothing wrong with them. And anyway, they are shipping today,'

'All the better for a quick decision, Mr Duc,'

'Where do I fit into this grand plan?'

With years of close acquaintance of my formidable business CV, Rocket had begun to pick up the scent. If Mr Duc's face showed a dollop of worry, Rod's bespoke a deluge.

I lay my plan out to them with the authority of a general planning an heroic charge at the enemy cannon. I explained that the 60,000 men's leather shoes were supposed to be dark brown, stitched with a light brown. I figured there were grounds for repudiation of the contract if I maintained that the thread was too pink. Mr Duc laughed and said I was taking too much medication. In reply, I bade Mr Duc and Rocket contemplate how many variations of light brown there were in the colour chart. The chart by the way, was owned by one of my competitors who was currently in Hanoi trying to close a deal on canvas slippers. Mr Duc had met my competitor's manager at a cafe that morning and secured the chart for a small incentive.

It was time to give Rocket his briefing. 'I will introduce you as the quality control inspector who has flown here to inspect the shoes on behalf of the German buyer. When you find the colour variation you reject the whole shipment. Simple as that.'

'No way,' Rocket replied. 'I have no idea about inspecting shoes. I lob for a holiday and here I am, en route to some factory where I am supposed to reject 60,000 pairs of shoes, based on pink thread. No way, mate.'

I held firm. 'You've got your business cards. Remember, you represent the buyer and you're a quality control inspector. I'll do all the talking. You just agree.'

A little disoriented from the heat and his hangover, Rod relented. He would give his support on the basis that he only had to nod and not speak.

Mac pulled into the factory where Mr Thay was looking very pleased with himself that his factory was finally running at full capacity twenty four hours a day.

The Smiling Assassin, I thought, as I lunged forward to shake his hand and convey good wishes to him and his family.

The introduction of Mr Rodney Cuthbertson, the quality control inspector, arrived last night from London, was met with concern by Mr Thay.

'Very pleased you come so far to my factory but today we ship.'

Mr Thay's smile made you feel like extracting each and every tooth.

'Well, Mr Thay,' I said, 'there is a small problem.' I then explained how the samples sent to the buyer had been rejected on the basis of colour of thread. On cue, Mr Duc produced the colour chart and pointed to the colour that should have been used, at the same time holding up one of the offending shoes. Mr Thay put on his glasses, compared the colours, looked to Rocket and said, 'I cannot see any difference in these colours, you must accept the shipment.'

So far Rocket had not said a word, just nodded in the right places. Now he looked at me with the fear of Samuel Goldwyn's Babylonians just before the Red Sea swallowed them.

I came to the rescue. 'I believe the word Mr Rodney is looking for is CANCELLATION.'

Mr Thay rushed from the meeting room and returned minutes later with six men who looked like factory hands. In reality they were his board — all high-paid government officials. As Mr Duc explained the situation in Vietnamese, the directors would from time to time cast looks in the direction of Mr Thay. These looks resembled those a home owner reserves for a dog messing his lawn. Quite clearly, the onus was on Mr Thay to solve this impasse.

So far so good. Even Rocket was starting to look more confident as he ran his WELL trained eye over the shoes, supposedly looking for even more mistakes. Mr Thay first offered tea to Mr Rodney as a pacifier, then took me aside and asked me to remember our long and fruitful relationship. He then asked me to consider the situation 'from the heart'.

This was too much. The time had come to release the rabid monkey from within my soul. 'Mr Thay, you tell me to consider from my heart. I have no heart. You have torn out my heart and thrown it on the road of your factory. Truck upon truck carrying the orders of my competitors have driven over my heart splashing my blood over your factory walls. And you say, consider from my heart!'

Pavarotti would have been proud of the crescendo I had reached.

Rocket's face looked like one of those clowns

you shove balls into at the Easter Show. Mr Duc was shaking his head and whispering to Rocket, 'Fucking unbelievable, very Shakespeare, fucking unbelievable.'

As it appeared I was very angry, the confused directors set upon Mr Thay. He skulked over to me.

'How can we solve this matter where we all be very happy?'

I quickly seized the moment. 'Well, Mr Thay, there is this other matter about the late delivery of 600,000 pair of sports shoes. I am sure that if you were able to complete them on time, I might be able to convince Mr Rodney to accept the men's leather shoes, even though they are a mistake.'

After a few brief words to the directors, Mr Thay gave me that smile again. 'Of course, I am sure we can complete as contracted.'

We could have left the meeting then and there. Mr Thay and his directors would have expected me to do a snow job on the inspector from London and that would have been that.

But Rocket, looking even more relaxed now I seemed to be off the hook, piped up. 'I suppose now that I'm here, I should inspect some shoes.'

It was like somebody had fired a hot-glue gun down my spine. I glared at Rocket with a look that said 'You idiot!' Here we were, just about to skip away from disaster and Rocket had to go and open that big mug of his. If Rocket had to answer a technical question from Mr Thay or his directors, we were in deep shit. Christ, I thought to myself, Rocket's only experience with footwear was getting lost in the shoe section at K-Mart. He has worn two types of shoes in his life — footy boots and thongs.

Before I could tell Mr Thay none of this was necessary, Mr Thay said, 'I will lead the way. It is only a short drive.'

Back in the Merc, Mac was asleep and the inside of the car a sauna.

'Rocket, what got into you for Christ's sake? We had the deal sown up, we were out of there!'

'Mate, I'm a bloody quality control inspector who has just flown all the way from London to solve this problem, the least I can do is take a geek at the shithouse shoes!'

I told Rocket to head for the car and have Mac ready for a quick getaway. Mr Duc had already started.

Mr Duc looked at me and made a serious situation ridiculous by saying, 'He has a point.'

Great. Here was Rocket believing he really was a quality control inspector and Mr Duc sharing the fantasy. I turned on Mr Duc.

'You were a great help in there. What were you gibbering about to the directors?'

'I told them Mr Rodney was famous. An expert at his job who would never make a mistake. They said the shipment was already on the dock about to be loaded.'

So that was where we were headed, the dock, with Mr Thay and the directors leading the way on their Honda Dream II's — the most prestigious mode of transport for the well-healed Vietnamese.

We looked like some diplomatic cavalcade and I prayed nobody took potshots at the Merc.

We finally came upon a huge holding yard. The entrance seemed official and Naval, and I thought it strange we proceeded without stopping at the checkpoint. The seven Hondas halted in front of a stack of forty-foot long containers.

'Not a fucking word this time, Inspector Holmes,' I hissed at Rocket as we got out and joined Mr Thay, who was pointing at the top container in a stack of three.

As I was wondering how were we going to check that, the biggest fork-lift I had ever seen lurched around the corner. It was like the T-Rex in *Jurassic Park*, though probably older and more dangerous. One of the directors nearly got himself squished as he stopped the machine and began some negotiation with the driver. Shortly thereafter, the driver brought the container from its position to a gentle rest in front of our anxious faces. Though one of us was looking more than just anxious. With the dawning of the task that would now befall him, Rocket had gone white and waxy, like something from Madame Tussaud's House of Horrors that had been left too long in the tropics.

The directors used a pair of wire clippers to break the seal on the container — technically a case of breaking and entering — opened the doors and pulled out several boxes of shoes. As they were placed on the ground in front of Rocket, the tension was palpable.

At that moment, I turned and noticed several well-armed navy personnel moving briskly towards us in a threatening manner.

Shit, things were turning ugly.

I put two and two together and came up with five, as one always does in Vietnam. I reckoned we were on a Naval base that acted as a secure storage area for containers pending shipping. Mr Thay and his directors had punted on there not being too many bods around during lunch hour, and those that were, being easily persuaded with 'sleeping pills' as described in local vernacular.

But now the business was getting out of hand. We were trespassing, breaking and entering and bribing.

I told Rocket to head for the car and have Mac ready for a quick getaway. Mr Duc had already started.

Mr Thay had not yet spotted the impending

problem. With one of his own style smiles, I advised Mr Thay that Mr Rodney had decided, upon my recommendation, to accept the shoes and allow shipment today. Mr Thay winked knowingly and said he would look into completing my sports shoes immediately.

As I reached the Merc, the smile was vanishing from Mr Thay's face. He had seen what was heading his way and knew he was in serious sewerage.

Mac put his foot to the floor and we sped away, intact and indeed triumphant.

For a long time Rocket sat in the Merc, still silent, obviously pondering the strange nature of the first four hours of his holiday. Eventually he looked at me and said, 'So where are we going for lunch?'

I said, 'Well there are these winter jackets I bought for a Russian client. On arrival in Slovenia they turned out to be rejects. I need you to come along to a lunch meeting and ...'

DAVE WARNER

AUSTRALIA 2

That September when we watched the sleek-hulled
   pride of Australia
Humble the Yanks and make Connor a failure
How our voices rose as one 'cross the breadth of
   the nation
Cans zipped, stubbies sipped, champagne corks
   popped in celebration.
But as our first minister, luridly dressed, blest the
   quest and its happy completion
We felt the deflation and frustration that we
   could not grant this joy its due consummation.

Then into this tempest of despair blew a positive
   air:
Somewhere in our rollicking midst
was the object, the vessel, the sacred ship!
A prize for the man who could follow it through
He'd win the hand of Australia 2

Like water through a holed hull we gushed,
I and ten thousand others joining the crush
As we scanned for a sign of that virgin yacht
From harbour to sandhill to city block.
Till by fate I was led to a revelling bar
Where big bosomed women with thighs ajar
Wearing nought but spangly bikinis and thongs
swung upside down singing national songs.
One former flapper, floppy and fat,
Conducted the choir with Bradman's bat,
Sailors, salesmen, welders and builders
Turned red noses skyward, sang 'Waltzing
    Matilda'
Eagerly straining for the rivers of piss
That flowed earthward from these harpies 'lips
And it marked as a man he who could catch
in his mouth the streams that flowed from their
    thatch.
Drunk on this communal brew I turned, I froze
I examined the mirror
That held the visage of our marine Madonna
Serenely sipping, slipped away from her crew
I sidled up to Australia 2

Her sleek skin gleamed in a radiant glow
And her fair hair shone on its kevlar bows
She asked me, How did I find her?
Dropped her shoulder revealing her starboard
    grinder
I, trembling, around it placed my hands

Felt her ballast shift,yes I was the man
The fortunate, chosen one, privileged one who
Would join the loins of Australia 2
With the spirited gum of his personal glue.
She heeled pointing high, I kissed her salt face
She invited me for a percolated coffee at her
    place.

Well, what a monument to national fervour
From the whitegum chairs to kangaroo berber
Men At Work on the stereo, Mike Walsh on the
    ceiling
Authentic sunburned coloured walls, zinc-creamed
    and self-peeling
Colonnades shaped like Bondi lifesavers
Supporting a cupola with a mural of Laver,
Nolan sketches, Bert Bryant tips, torn and ripped
    and trapped in the floorboards,
Each etched with the features of a true-Aussie
    warlord,
Gumless Graham, sleeveless Hoges, gormless
    Gunston
And in the wardrobe Lillee's sweat-caked
    headband
An ARIA head band's head-job
Snapped, freeze-framed beside Newcombe's
    winning Wimbledon lob

To the soft-lit chamber was I led
And placed in a beer-bottle shaped waterbed

Where beneath the doona from Koala Blue
I fondled the stern of Australia 2.

Ah ecstacy! Words cannot grasp
the pleasures my hands did when they held the
  brass
of my sweet sensitive companion's
Glamourous, glabrous, stays and stanchions
My fingers crawled up inside her spinnaker,
  unfastened the kite
I held fast my lips to the precious ship's side
And my loins surged
There was but one space to conquer
She read my thoughts
Swayed and weighed anchor
She presented it to me
She coyly revealed
The mystic, magnificent, wings of her keel.
What had taken Ben Lexcen so long to originate
I strove and drove and thrust to invaginate
To me had fallen the task to anoint
The arcane, perfect pleasure point
And though sharp polyps slashed at my genitals
Yet I would not halt my nuptial ritual
And no barnacled bar would prevent me anew
From repeating that beat with Australia 2
I could not resist the wooing and wedding
The kissing and cuddling, the crewing and
  bedding
And no barnacled bar would prevent me anew

From repeating that beat with Australia 2
For I fastened my name to history with glue
The night I f*****
Australia 2

LIBBY-JANE CHARLESTON

REDHEADS

I'm not afraid of death but I'm afraid of dancing. My last girlfriend was a terrific dancer. She had a tango ability at birth. She had good rhythm, while I stomp and stamp on the dance floor. I pull at my trousers and wave my arms. I try to strike up conversations with the DJ. 'Is Fleetwood Mac planning a reunion?' I'd say. Everybody yells at me when I request unfashionable songs. 'Legs ... ZZTop?' I beg. I do the chicken dance. Everybody laughs at me and calls me a spastic. 'You're such a spastic,' they say, as they shine under the disco ball. But there will soon be a day when small-minded people become giants and even the best dancers will finally dry up and blow away.

I work on the third floor of a building famous because the architect who designed it shot dead an eighty-two year old man and shouted, 'I'm a natural born killer!' His killing spree ended when he shot a teenage girl who'd given the wrong answer to his question, 'Do you feel distraught when you hear Kurt Cobain sing?'

My office is only two blocks away from the sandwich shop where my sister works. Sometimes I watch her window-shopping on her lunchbreak. One day I thought it would be fun to throw something at her as she passed below my window. I took a battery out of my Walkman and dropped it but my aim was off and I hit somebody else. Somehow the man suffered concussion and the police were sent up to investigate. When they asked me if I knew anything about dangerous objects being thrown from windows I said, 'My secretary has been acting strangely.' They took her to the station and questioned her until she broke down and confessed to a string of trivial robberies. She also admitted she was plotting revenge against a teenager who'd gotten her pregnant. 'Why don't people believe American sailors are capable of brutality?' she said.

It's been nearly two months since I've had sex. Instead, I've been watching lots of late night television. I've been enjoying re-runs of 'Prisoner' and spend hours thinking about women with blue overalls and uncombed hair. If I'm having difficulty getting to sleep I walk the lonely acres of my apartment and fantasise about women behind bars. Lately even the elderly cast members are starting to look good.

My boss is eager for me to get married. He says nobody really trusts a single man and I tell him, 'I'm having trouble meeting the right girl.' He tells me to join a dating agency and later he leaves some pamphlets on my desk. I make an appointment to join 'Direct Contacts'.

I ignore the memo on my desk advising me to attend a meeting with a stockbroker. Instead I meet a client for lunch, who is trying to sue a clairvoyant for telling her she was, and always will be, a hussy. We order red wine and fish. The client is fat and makes it clear from the start she doesn't want to talk business. She is wearing a short white skirt and tells

I tell the secretary to hold all my calls and I watch Rikki Lake, Donahue and Oprah. Not only does this kill lots of time, but I get to see people worse off than me.

me I remind her of her ex-husband, 'because you both hide behind thick glasses'. I'm trying to tell her about our latest case and she's intent on finding more similarities — 'you both speak with a Melbourne twang' and 'I bet you both jam up talkback radio'. Later she cries into her wine and says her ex-husband never really loved her, 'except in the same way West Australians love playing Lotto'. On the way back to work I have my hair cut. My hair no longer touches my shoulders. It's the same style I had when I was nineteen. Don't you always go back to the haircut you had when you were most happy?

When I get back to the office I lock my door and turn on my television. I tell the secretary to hold all my calls and I watch Rikki Lake, Donahue and Oprah. Not only does this kill lots of time, but I get to see people worse off than me. After three hours I can see my life beginning to flower. I saw an episode about a woman who had lost four children to drug abuse. She said, 'It feels like I'm raining inside.'

I get my first date through the dating agency. There is a message on my answering machine from a woman called Jenny. She sounds very happy when I ring her. 'I love music, good wine, great conversation and water sports.' We agree to meet at a popular bar. I am disappointed to see she is a redhead. She doesn't let go of her handbag all night and tells me she knows lots about Aboriginal culture.

'I went out with a man called Mungawindi,' she says. She keeps touching her left ear and tries to impress me with her knowledge of everything Chinese. 'Chiang Kai-shek survived the most amazing kidnapping in history!' Halfway through dinner she kisses me on the cheek and asks me what turns me on. I tell her, 'There were moments last year when I was full of spit and fire but now all I crave is financial stability and a sunshine-filled consciousness.' She looks puzzled. Later I tell her I had a nice night and yes of course I will call you. The next day I phone the dating agency and told them off for setting me up with a nutcase. 'What are you, a cave dweller?' said the receptionist.

My boss comes into my office to tell me I've been doing a good job. He tells me I'm an asset to the company. 'You're our golden boy,' he says. I tell him I've already had one date through the dating agency and he looks quite pleased. At the last office party he had too much to drink and told everybody he can only get an erection near an open window. He said he was struck down by this strange affliction on the day his grandmother mysteriously went blonde. 'It happened overnight,' he'd said.

At home there is a message from a girl called Lynette. 'I'm twenty-eight and really wild,' she says. I phone her and we agree to meet for a drink. She is a redhead. I'm wondering if this is just a coincidence and make a mental note to tell the dating agency I'd prefer a variety. We drink beer and she rests her hand on my thigh.

'Describe to me the making of a perfect banana split,' she says.

I take this as a come-on and invite her to my apartment for dinner. I promise to cook apricot chicken and she follows me to my kitchen. Later she takes off her clothes and spends several minutes explaining that the hideous red growth covering half of her body is nothing more sinister than a birthmark. I say 'Okay,' and turn out the light.

In the dark I make-believe she's the older sister of a school friend who died in the Luna Park ghost train fire. At his funeral she'd said to me, 'I hope your death is bloody and unexpected,' and I've been reading romantic things into it ever since.

At work the next day I find several urgent faxes on my desk. Somebody has spilt something orange on my carpet and I ask the secretary if she's been using my office. She tells me she'd have to be pretty bored to step foot into my office and 'Don't you know boredom is the lowest depth of misery?' she says. Someone has left a Fred Flintstone coffee mug on my desk. I throw it out the window and call the dating agency.

'Stop sending me redheads!' I say. I tell the receptionist I just want blondes and brunettes. The manager gets on the phone and says 'Do you have a preference for permed hair?'

She thinks she is very funny. When I get home there is a message from someone called Donna. Her voice is deep and husky.

'Tell me about yourself,' I ask. She tells me she has been divorced twice and now she's just looking for a good time. She tells me she loves the smooth sounds of Shirley Bassey and she hopes Hugh Grant will finally be given a break. When she asks about me I tell her there are so many spiders in my flat I'm forced to arm myself with a broom. I tell her I truly believe Sylvester Stallone is a misunderstood genius.

I meet her at my favourite bar and I'm shocked to see she's a redhead! I tell her something very serious has just come up and I have to leave. I almost run out the door and she's yelling behind me, 'But I've already ordered you a Grasshopper!'

The next day I meet a client who wants to sue his boss for telling people he looks like Hitler. I tell him he has no grounds for defamation and surely it's not the first time somebody has pointed out the similarity?

'Hell, I don't even have a moustache,' he said, and that night I dream of Hitler's jackboots strutting around my balcony.

My boss tells me I should take a holiday. He says I'm not looking my vibrant self.

> *i* leave the room in a hurry because, in my experience, heated discussion inevitably leads to sex.

'Any luck with women?' he asks. I tell him the agency keeps sending me redheads and it's starting to drive me crazy. I tell him I'm very fussy, I'm looking for Miss Perfect.

'I make life tough for anyone sharing my bed,' I say. My secretary is eavesdropping. She says she had no idea I was desperate enough to join a dating agency.

'I could introduce you to some of my girlfriends,' she said. She acts insulted when I ask her if she is friends with any women who finished high school. She's so angry with me she leaves an elastic band in my coffee and when I tell her she can leave early she says, 'You are like every man who says looks don't matter and then you drag out the issue of IQ, like some stinking mullet.' I leave the room in a hurry because, in my experience, heated discussion inevitably leads to sex.

The boss calls an urgent meeting to say somebody has been stealing from the company's social club funds.

'We now have exactly thirty-five cents towards our Christmas party,' he says. He also says somebody has been throwing things out of the window and 'Pedestrians have been complaining'. My secretary winks at me and for the first time I notice she's losing a battle with acne.

The dating agency manager returns my call. 'We do not deliberately give you redheads,' says the manager. She tells me everyone is matched according to compatibility.

'You've listed your hobbies as golf, cooking and drinking. Each woman we've matched you with has listed similar pursuits,' she explains. When I get home there is a message from a woman called Karen. I arrange to meet her for a drink. I notice her hair is auburn.

'Would you call yourself a redhead?' I asked.

'Yes, I suppose I would,' she said.

'Goodbye,' I said.

It seems a higher power is sending frogs and locusts to punish me.

At home there is a message from a woman called Jenny, demanding to know why she hasn't heard from me. 'Is it something I said?' she moans.

There is another message from a woman called Susan. She is very happy to hear from me. She says, 'This singles scene is scary!' We spent a few moments on small talk. I told her my health is good, my secretary is practically illiterate and my hair is dark brown.

'How about you?' I asked.

'I'm a natural blonde,' she said.

We arrange to meet the next night for drinks. I spend the day dictating letters to my secretary who is overexcited because she'd spent the night with the son of a famous singer.

'He told me I was the most glamourous girl in the pub!' I told her glamour is very different from beauty and 'The poor guy was probably wearing his beer goggles.' She's so upset she leaves the room and I can hear her crying in the bathroom. I stand outside the door and yell 'Stop grooming yourself!' and I laugh so hard I have to loosen my tie.

I have lunch with a particularly pesky client who wants to sue a religious cult because they talked her into posing naked for a photograph that eventually became a famous album cover.

'I don't even like the band,' she said.

She tells me she has an Asian sugar daddy and when I call her a whore she says, 'But don't you realise every Australian politician has one too?' I order spinach fettucine and she asks for a taste.

'No, I don't like sharing my food,' I say and she is so angry she leaves without paying and finds another lawyer to handle her case. When I tell my boss I've been dumped by a client because I wouldn't let her try my pasta he says

'None of us ever really finishes with childhood.'

My secretary sneaks out of work early so I follow her to the train station. I'm hoping she won't suddenly turn around and see me. I stand behind her in the queue to buy a ticket and just when she's about to step onto the train I tap her shoulder and yell, 'Where the hell are you going?' and she's so terrified she screams. I let her go and I even wave to her as the train carries her to god-knows-where. I turn to the stationmaster who'd seen the whole thing and I say, 'My secretary is always sneaking out early,' and he nods like it's something he's put up with for years.

I decide to leave early too and walk home from the station. I have a long shower and put on my best clothes. I've got a good feeling about tonight's date. Susan was also the name of a woman I'd kissed at one hell of a party six years ago. I started practicing witty things to say to her like 'Celibacy is an overrated virtue' and 'Did you know Charles Bronson used to be a coal miner?' and 'Jack Kevorkian is going to make a guest appearance on 'ER'!'

I tell her I'm doing this for her own good, for my own good, for the good of the company. I tell her I'm going to shave her head.

I get to the bar half an hour early and drink

two glasses of wine to calm my nerves. A woman comes up to me and says, 'Are you alone?' and I can't believe my luck, it must be the drawing power of my pale purple shirt. I tell her, 'Well, I'm kind of waiting for someone,' and she walks away. Suddenly I feel a soft hand on my shoulder and I look up and she says, 'Hi, I'm Susan' and I'm in utter shock because her hair is red and I lose control and start shaking her and I yell, 'You're a liar, you're a liar!'

The next day at work the secretary isn't at her desk. I visit the accountant's secretary to see if she knows where the stupid girl could be. 'She's getting some milk, I think,' she says.

An hour later I can hear her on the phone so I use the intercom to call her into my office.

'I'm coming,' she says and hell, this can't be happening, but her hair is red ...

I am very calm, I say 'What have you done to your hair?' and she says 'What does it look like? I dyed it. I wanted a change,' and I order her to stay in the office.

'If you leave this room, you'll be sacked, get it?' I say.

I sprint to the chemist and buy a packet of razors. When I get back to the office the secretary is still sitting on the desk. She doesn't look terrified. She has no idea what's going to happen. I tell her this isn't going to hurt. I tell her I'm doing this for her own good, for my own good, for the good of the company. I tell her I'm going to shave her head.

'But before I do, I'm going to tell you a story.'

A magician invites an audience member to hit him on the head with an axe. To the horror of everyone watching, his skull splits open and his body hits the floor. The magician is rushed to hospital, where he is subjected to emergency brain surgery. But, alas, he slips into a coma. Five months go by. No sign of life. Six months. Nothing. Then the doctor summons the magician's family to his bedside. He says, 'It's time for you to make a decision.' Suddenly, the magician's nostrils flare, his eyes spring open and he jumps out of bed shouting, 'I tricked you!'

STEVE BEDWELL

MORE BITS AND PIECES

THE PARTY

Last night was a terrific party.
There were plenty of amphetamines and hallucinogens.
There were abundant barbiturates and no strings attached group sex.
Cheryl also brought a lovely sponge that her mother had made.

CRACKER NIGHT

I'll never forget Cracker Night, 1978.

My cross Alsatian, Tarsha, frightened, escaped through a hole in the fence.

Run over by a Hillman Minx, she has suffered hip dysplasia ever since.

Maybe dad was right, perhaps locking her in the laundry because she gets frightened wouldn't have been so cruel after all.

THE RSL CLUB

The busy RSL Club has it all.

The busy RSL Club has snooker and darts.

The busy RSL Club has poker machines and a bistro.

The busy RSL Club has a happy man with a red face and a bow tie on the door who works the public address system.

Bugger, it's me who's left their headlights on.

BARRY COHEN

WHEN THE LIGHTS WENT OUT

The First Lady was knocked cold last week by an elephant. Well that's not quite correct. She was knocked out by a cat and an elephant. Bear with me.

Those of you who are familiar with the good lady, Rae, and my occasional scribblings will be aware that she is mildly eccentric. As the Dame would say, 'I mean that in the nicest possible way'. Her little quirks and obsessions are what makes her both interesting and lovable. Mind you as with all eccentrics, she doesn't see anything unusual in her behaviour. Nothing she does is dangerous to her friends, family or her good self. Up until now that is. A little background is essential.

We live increasingly alone, as the offspring hive off to nests of their own, in a small farmlet in

Matcham on the Central Coast of NSW. For those unfamiliar with Matcham I should point out that it is two woods and a five iron to Terrigal. Together, with number two son Martin, we live an idyllic rustic existence with a goat, donkey, Shetland pony, two wallaroos, two shetland sheepdogs and two cats. It would not be overstating the case to suggest that were it not for the First Lady their numbers would be markedly less. As a former Environment Minister I am not overly impressed with the blood-bespattered remains of native fauna that are regularly dropped on our lounge room floor by the feline members of the family. All very interesting I hear you say, but what in the name of all that's holy does that have to do with elephants. Patience, dear readers. All will be revealed.

Quarantine regulations alone ensured that no elephants joined our menagerie at Matcham.

To further follow this bizarre tale, you should be aware of the beloved's current obsession with folkcraft. Some two dozen moons or so ago she turned her considerable artistic talents to various forms of patchwork, quilting, tatting, embroidery and the like. Our modest rural abode now resembles an eastern seraglio to the point where anyone can fall and land uninjured on a cushion. And now to the elephant.

There are not many things that the First Lady has in common with John Elliot, formerly of Fosters and Liberal Party fame. She detests beer and is not all that keen about Liberals either. However they share one great passion — elephants.

It all started, for the First Lady that is, a decade or so ago when, like all good Labor folk, we were on safari in Kenya and in the process drove through the middle of a herd of six hundred elephants. Quarantine regulations alone ensured that no elephants joined our menagerie at Matcham. Inside our rural retreat, however, the place is awash with the buggers. They range from gall-stone size to life-like replicas and adorn every mantelpiece, shelf, ledge and precipice available. A giant of solid teak sat in the family room on the roll-top desk, a mere foot or two above where she nightly quilts and watches the telly.

On the third of April, as the rest of the nation noisily celebrated my birthday, the Cohen family supped well at a local restaurant. It was excellent fare, washed down with a precocious little Pinot Noir. Those who know me well will accept my assurance that one bottle shared between four was all that was consumed.

The night was still young when we returned sober to Matcham.

Picture the scene. The very epitome of blissful

domesticity. Youthful grandparents relaxing with coffee and port, content that yet another day had passed without incident. Short of an earthquake it was hard to imagine either of us coming to grief. It was then that it happened.

Suddenly, without so much as a by-your-leave, the younger of the cats, Nelson, did his version of a whirling dervish. Leaping from atop the elephant he threw himself into the air while simultaneously kicking backwards with his hind legs. With growing horror I watched the elephant slide off the desk-top and sail gracefully through the air before landing with a sickening thud on the First Lady's head.

Our eyes met briefly, then hers rolled around like poker machine tumblers and closed. She slid gracefully off the couch. Nary a sound passed her lips. The elephant, on the other hand, continued on its merry way, spraying coffee all over her latest quilting masterpiece.

She would, had she been conscious, been proud of my lightning reaction. In a split second I was beside her. However, what does one do then? I had never seen her look so peaceful. I checked all the things I could think of checking and came to the conclusion she was out cold.

Should I ring for an ambulance or a doctor? Stretched out on the sofa, she could hardly be more comfortable. Three or four minutes elapsed before she shuddered, moaned and, not surprisingly, clasped her head. 'Darling,' I cried, 'are you all right?' What else can one say at moments like these? Ignoring my solicitations, barely conscious and swaying, she staggered to the sink clutching the coffee-stained quilt and commenced sponging it clean.

'A year of my life has gone into this,' she cried.

Now why would anyone think she's eccentric.

DAVID DALE

BANANA APPEAL

It is with the greatest reluctance that I stand here and cast the first stone at the Bananas in Pyjamas. They are, after all, national icons — the financial saviours of the ABC and Australia's cultural ambassadors to the world. They have the undying gratitude of parents who know they can leave their children in front of a Banana video without fear that the kids will end up ninja-kicking their playmates or demanding junk foods by brand name.

I expect that in the year 2002, the Bananas will be joint presidents of the republic. The messages they're imprinting on today's children will dominate Australian thinking in the 21st century. That's why we have to watch them carefully.

It's only when you try to think of alternatives

to Bananas in Pyjamas that you realise what a perfectly calculated product they are. Other marketing opportunities from the vegetable kingdom may come to mind, but you will quickly find reasons to reject them: Zucchinis in Bikinis (too sexy), Beans in Jeans (too casual), Passionfruits in Bathing suits (see above), Jellies in Wellies (too English), Kippers in Slippers (too smelly), Peas on Skis (too fast), Pears in Flares (too 70s), Caulies with Brollies (too complicated).

It turns out the Bananas in Pyjamas are unique, a brilliant blend of wholesomeness and humour. No wonder they earn the ABC ten million dollars a year. But I'm beginning to fear that these giant fruits may be out of control, and that their influence on young Australian minds is not entirely benign.

My first experience of the power of the concept was back in 1993, at an ABC promotional event, when Andrew Olle and I were booed off stage by a gang of four-year-olds shouting, 'We want the Bananas'. Being booed off stage was hardly a new experience for me, but seeing such ignominy heaped upon Mr Integrity suggested this was a phenomenon with terrifying implications.

More recently my three-year-old daughter was bitten on the finger by a child named Navette (where do parents find these names?) during a struggle over a Banana in Pyjamas beanie at her kindergarten. Our household is not particularly

Banana-conscious. We have a few plastic figurines of the Bananas and their teddy neighbours (Morgan, Amy and Lulu). We have a doll with detachable pyjamas, two books, a T-shirt, a Lulu stamp which has put green ink over most of our furniture, four video collections of the TV episodes, and the aforementioned beanie.

Unlike a million other Australian households, we did not feel the need for Banana sheets, towels,

'I'm a rat, I'm a rat, I'm a clever, clever rat.'

backpack, pencil box, ruler, socks, or games. So far my daughter seems to have escaped the conditioning that drove Navette to violence in her desperation to own the complete Banana oeuvre.

The Bananas stories shown on ABC TV in the original five-minute episodes just before Playschool looked innocent enough. The early video collections have the teddies learning to count and read and share their toys, and being helped through difficulties by the Bananas, who seem to occupy all positions of authority on Cuddles Avenue (park rangers, beach patrol, erecting street signs, sweeping the roads, repairing cars, treating injuries — real renaissance fruits, in fact). A picky person might suggest that this discourages self-reliance among children, since they will grow up thinking that whenever they're in trouble a piece of fruit will step out and save them.

But I think there is more to worry right-thinking Australians in the more recent video collections, particularly in the attitudes to capitalism engendered by a character called Rat in a Hat. As a citizen of John Howard's Lucky Country, you naturally hold the view that the business of Australia is business. So does the Rat in a Hat. He runs all the businesses in Cuddles Avenue — a shoe shop, a paint shop, a cafe, a fairground, and a carpet warehouse. So for thousands of Australian children, he's their first (and formative) image of the entrepreneur.

And what does he do? Finding he's out of size six shoes, he puts size fours in a box labelled six and sells them to Morgan Teddy. Finding he's out of yellow paint, he re-labels a can of purple paint and sells it to Lulu Teddy. He sells Morgan a magic carpet that won't fly, and at his fairground, he fixes all the games so nobody can win a prize.

Even in his leisure time, the Rat is still selling. When his car breaks down, he manages to unload it on Amy Teddy in exchange for her scooter. And when the Bananas go on holidays, he persuades them to let him house-sit, getting free accommodation and eating their entire store of munchy honey cakes. Whenever the Bananas or the teddies express doubt about his offers, he says: 'Trust me, I'm a rat.' And when they fall for a scam, he walks away singing 'I'm a rat, I'm a rat, I'm a clever, clever rat.'

I imagine that the Rat character was added when the scriptwriters realised that every good story needs a villain. The early Bananas episodes had a certain blandness, because the only evils on display were vanity (Lulu), jealousy (Amy) and early morning grumpiness (Morgan).

The program was conceived in the late 1980s, when the rotten apples who had risen to the top of the capitalist barrel were still leaving a nasty taste. So it's hardly surprising that the writers, seeking a modern age villain who is non-violent but definitely sleazy and deep-down stupid, would come up with a rodent form of Christopher Skase.

Since free enterprise is totally different now, and children are the consumers of the future, the ABC needs a stern letter from the Business Council of Australia, and the Rat in a Hat needs to fall victim to a leveraged buy-out by the Teddies.

WÏLBUR WÏLDÉ

IT TOOK CANBERRA TO THINK OF IT

From the middle 1970s onwards I spent time touring Australia with a couple of well-known rock bands. It's a great way to see the country. People either welcome you with open limbs, bottles or mouths or they just get out of your way, whatever. Every now and then we went to Canberra. In fact my first-ever visit to our nation's capital was with Ol'55. It left a lasting impression. Outwardly the city represents all that is solid and sensible but dig deeply and you'll find a healthy subculture of insanity and self-expression. We did one crazy gig at the ANU Student Union building and also at CAE out past some really big roundabouts, where future leaders of our nation lay face down in roach-filled ashtrays still clutching the tequila bottle that helped put them there. Also on that trip we had Kombi trouble that led to me being at the wheel of said, dead wagon as it was towed home to Sydney by a rented truck, full of stage gear, at an average 137 kph on a rope as long as my dick plus four feet. The truck was driven by Dave, who was driven by Satan. When I was able to catch his eye in the side-mirror and wave him down to a more manageable pace he just waved back smiling. We arrived in town shortly with me visibly unnerved and almost visibly leaking. He apologised and promised his first-born son as retribution. It sounded reasonable at the time. His name is Ryan and he lives in our ceiling.

There was a nightclub in Canberra, above some shops, in a kind of mall sort of thing in a suburbish type of situation. Its name was 'The place where grown men and too few women drink too much booze before, during and after some mighty stomping gigs.' Canberra had a few of those joints that, along with the fine music enthusiasts and vain exponents, made for a healthy rock'n'roll scene all through the 1970s and 1980s, which brings me to the point of this yarn.

The year was 1982. The venue was the Bruce Sports Stadium, Canberra. The band was Dire Straits. The saxophone ring-in was me. Eight thousand punters had nestled in for a quality ACT evening with Mark Knopfler and the other guys. I'd been flown in from Melbourne to play on two songs, 'Local Hero' and 'Twistin' by the Pool'. The tapes had arrived ten days before, in time for me to learn my bits, although there was some contention about this at the sound-check when Knopface suggested that they sounded not

Also on that trip we had Kombi trouble that led to me being at the wheel of said, dead wagon as it was towed home to Sydney by a rented truck, full of stage gear, at an average 137 kph on a rope as long as my dick plus four feet.

like the way that Mike Brecker had played them on the record. The greatest saxophone player in the world, he assured me. I conceded that he was an all right player but Knophead couldn't leave it alone and made me go practice with the keyboardist, Tommy, who got me up to scratch in no time. We went to dinner all buddies, until I mentioned one of my roadie mates whom Knopfeatures also knew and happened to hate. Suffice to say, at this embryonic stage of our relationship, I'd not impressed Mr K one iota, except that I could fit my entire head up my own ass.

Showtime and under instruction from the tour manager, I took my entry position side-stage. I waited for my cue, ready to climb the stairs and move cat-like onto my mark alongside bassist, John Isley. Knopfler was in full flight. Flailing the bejesus out of a semi-acoustic, pouring his soul into the intro of his lilting, Gaelic-inspired 'Local Hero'. He played great stuff and, lit only by a single spotlight, really built the moment. The crowd was hushed, in awe of the guitar genius, digging the raw emotion that flowed like their pre-show cocktails. By now a convert, I was thinking this really is a terrific moment of creativity and I'm honoured to be part of it. The tap on the shoulder told me it was time to join in this sublime anticipation. After all it was the big hit tune from the big hit movie. Everything was perfect and Mr K was having a ball wallowing in the adulation. I sidled up to Mr Isley just as the majestic guitar feature wound down a tad before once again soaring, ever higher, to affect the desired climax and segue into the tune proper. Breathing into the mouthpiece to keep it warm and in tune, I stood in semi-darkness listening for the pick-up phrase at which point I would join in with my not the best in the world saxophone playing. It was about then that a couple of Canberrans near the front recognised me from gigs gone by and wanted me to notice them so they called out 'WOOBAH!!' I tried not to hear. Once again they yelled 'WOOBAH WIDE!!!! DAKTABONE!!!' It was pretty loud. In fact, quite audible to most of the audience and not a little disruptive given that by now Knopneck was throwing hideously contorted glances in my direction. In a bid to regain appropriate reverence, I raised one finger to my lips. It just seemed to create more raucousness, by virtue of me having acknowledged them, I suppose. They started cheering, others joined in, I suspect sensing the mischief.

Mr K played on but it was different. The flowing melodic lines were giving way to jagged, uneven slashing noises. We all owe Hendrix a great debt. Behind the first guys some others had taken up the cause for silence by telling everyone to 'SHUT UP!! WOOBAH SAYS QUIET!!!! NOOO!! LETS HEAR THE DAKTABONE!!! YEAH!!' It sounded like a weird, echoey, very public, domestic violence commercial. During the commotion I made some lame comment to Isley along the lines of 'one bad apple in the bunch' but he'd already thrown me to the wolves. I was cold and hungry. Knopfler had salvaged enough of his now tormented solo to still be in control of most of the punters, but the damage was done and those people shouting my name were responsible. Somehow his command of the crowd had been sabotaged. Guilty by association. Death. Rows 5 and 7 front right were yelling back to 10 and 11 'SIDDOWN AND SHUDDUP YOU WANKERS!!!' who replied by singing along and waving with only some of their fingers. As we started the tune proper it chilled out and they seemed to reach a kind of mid-show truce that, apart from a small flare-up in 'Twistin', my second appearance, lasted pretty much for the rest of the night. The après gig wind-down was understandably wintry, but trying to exonerate myself I felt kind of proud of my fellow countrymen who had been unafraid to welcome me back to their beautiful city. The guys in the band did a nice thing and invited me to fly with them to Sydney that night on their chartered Lear jet so I suppose there were no residual bad feelings.

Although it was my only gig with 'Dire Straits' I remember it fondly and I was sad to learn soon after that Mark Knopfler broke his arm in an Australian Grand Prix celebrity race. Distracted perhaps by some Canberran race fans yelling 'KNOPFLERRRYOUFUCKINGLE-GEND!!'

Now that's funny.

MAX CULLEN

THE MAGIC OF RESEARCH

He looks once more upon the Tom Bass relief atop the Sydney Morning Herald building entrance and decides it has, with time and resignation, improved.

Max Cullen, actor researching the role of news hound, runs his paw through thinning hair, tucks shirt in and bounds three steps to the past.

Last time he adjoined these hallowed columns was as a newspaper copyboy, starting a life apprenticeship. That was before the computer took charge making hundreds of people redundant, when a copyboy might hand-deliver a front page scoop from courthouse to news-stand — every step of the way. It didn't make you feel especially important, but there was a kind of pride in

being a link in the chain of something —
important.

Cullen has long since broken with such
important stuff, taken up acting and, with an
audition coming up next week, has a good
chance of being cast as legendary knock-about
journalist Sean Gavelkind in the upcoming flick,
Life and Time.

To get it right, our consummate actor has made
an appointment to see an old journo who knew
Sean Gavelkind. Glen MacArthy sounded a mite
terse on the phone, but agreed to spare a few
minutes because he likes Max's acting 'sometimes'.

We are handed a scrap of yellow copy paper:

A

Life

Is a coin

Spinning on edge

Not ours to spend –

A

Lend

Coined

Like a word

In this sentence.

'One of Gavel's arrow poems,' explains Glen
MacArthy, a vigorous spirited newspaper man
trapped in a large, lumbering, worn-out, old
body, '— found it stuck in his desk after he shot
through on us.'

MacArthy is the chief subeditor of the *Sydney Morning Herald*, he gave Sean Gavelkind — 'Marc Thyme' as he was known then — his first by-line. He is sitting with Max in a quiet corner of the newsroom leafing through press clippings in a manila folder. Glen is about as close to complete retirement as anyone could be — the original yellow journalist, complexion of uncooked pumpkin scone, with currants. Nevertheless, the flow of his commentary is unfaltering and articulate, as with controlled pride and masked enthusiasm he eulogises parent-like upon the merits of the wayward scribe.

'People say Sean was nothing but a bum, a drunkard, a womanising bastard with no depth of feeling except when it came to wallowing in self-pity — that's just unexpurgated fucking bullshit. He was a fine writer and humanitarian t'boot.'

He shows Max an unpublished piece written by a youthful Sean.

'Here's an example: the chief sub at the time dropped this piece, "defamatory", he called it — I nicked it from the waste bin — it'll give you a clue to Gavel's Gaelic style. Read it aloud to me, actor, I'd like to hear you read it.'

We oblige: 'A most sobering thought for any journalist is that what was news today is history tomorrow and whatever they deign to write lives on — under the lino in Grandma's house, folded away inside the sweatband of Uncle Bill's old hat, on a nail in the dunny, or on microfilm in the Mitchell Library ...

'And nowadays CD-ROM,' ad libs the actor.

'Just read,' prompts scone with a scowl.

' ... History will show that Les Mullins was a "good" journo, someone said so at his cremation. He leaves behind three ex-wives, two sons, a daughter, and one tearful de facto overheard to comment, "I didn't know the bastard had any friends."

'She was partly right, Les Mullins was hated by countless avid readers of his daily column, nevertheless, staunch work mates admired his rugged individuality, inflexibility of opinion and capacity for drink.'

'That's true,' says MacArthy, interrupting Max in full flow.

'Do you want me to keep reading?'

'Keep reading.'

'"Someone has to write an obit for Les," croaked Jim-the-grub and looked at me. "Ah, harrr! you knew him less longer than any of us, Gravelpit, you do it." Jim-the-grub likes to call people funny names and talk improper English, he also does not tub too much but is good at his job when he has to be chief sub because he know how to delete — and such.

'"Should I interview his ... widow?" I venture, incognisant of the politically correct mode of addressing an aggrieved whore.

'"What the hell for," he says, lighting a new cigarette from a half-smoked one. "She wouldn't know him."

*L*es Mullins never knocked back a drink, never left a glass till it was empty, always knew when it was his shout, and never, ever, ever owed nobody nothin'.

'I took an early tea break and lurched pub wards. I had a couple of days to write the piece. I am on a Sunday paper, permanent casual feature writer, Sean Gavelkind is my name, I sign my stuff Marc Thyme.

'A "Your shout, Gavel!" came from a crowd of mourners maintaining the vigil of Mullins's wake at the SPORTSMAN'S BAR — a pet meeting place for scribes who had long ago debated and argued the toss as to whether SPORTSMAN'S or SPORTSMENS' was correct — it was Les who umpired the final decision: "Sportsman is always plural, like soldier or reporter. Any man who is part of a team is never alone." Les never argued, he just stated facts.

'"To Les," we said in scattered unison.

'"— a true mate," added Big Harry Leith. And we all emptied our glasses. Another round was quickly dressed along the bar and Judy the barmaid held her hands up defensively — "No," she said. "This round's on me, I knew Les too,

171

you know. I was probably in love with him once — dunno for sure — but here's to him, he was a man."

'Talking to Big Harry later, privately, I inquire what sort of bloke he thought Les Mullins was really — fraternal loyalty aside.

'"I don't bag my mates, son," he said fraternally. "We're a brotherhood in this business — would you bag your brother?"

'I decided I probably would and didn't answer.

'Smith stuck his pug-nose in "What's the argument?"

'Big Harry affected a sneer "Marc Thyme wants to rake some mud up and cast it at Les's memory."

'"I've got to write a little piece about him for Sunday, that's all — a few lines about what a good bloke he was, or whatever,"

'"That's easy," boasted the pug-nose, puffing himself out some more, "Just say: Les Mullins never knocked back a drink, never left a glass till it was empty, always knew when it was his shout, and never, ever, ever owed nobody nothin'."

'"That was beaudeeful, Smiddy," blubbered Harry and a tear fell down his cheek.

'Back in the office I scanned the Mullins file — the lifetime he had worked for the press. His by-line was there when Darwin was bombed by the Japs and when Tracy blew it away, he was there when the North Shore Harbour Bridge was opened in 1932 and when the Tasman Bridge was knocked down in 1975. I took a trip to his old desk and stood there looking at it for ten minutes; I couldn't sit in his chair because he was still there — squinting through smoke from the butt in his tight lips — hunched over a deadline, pausing briefly to say, "I liked your piece on Sunday, Sean. Good stuff."

'"I thank you," I said out loud, and the place was empty again.

'One of the cleaners was pushing one of those big sacks of scrap down the hallway, he stopped and had a look and spoke –

'"Sad about Mr Mullins."

'"Yeah," I said.

'"Goodnight."

'"Goodnight."

'It was no coincidence that a few hours later I was drinking with Les's eldest son Bob in the Texas Tavern: it was one of few places open at ungodly hours. We didn't say much. Les filled the pauses.'

MacArthy and Cullen sit in silence for a moment, the Chief-sub, out of respect, the actor, because he doesn't have a script. However, he does have an old stand-up routine which he will now give an airing.

'Ah, yes — er ... the legendary newspaperman ... a "Newspaperman" — now, that's a silly bloody expression, isn't it? — so's this.'

Max pulls a silly facial expression. Glen frowns.

'Newspaperman. You sort of imagine a person who is flat, oblong, and limp — don't you — sort of yellow and wrapped around a bottle (laughing), with lots and lots of words coming out of him ... newspaperman —

'My dad was a newspaperman.

'(Serious.) We picked him up off the lawn every morning. He was always getting ripped — reckoned he had printers ink in his blood — funny that — smelled just like Irish whisky with a beer chaser. Mum reckoned she could read Dad like a book. The time he turned up with page three written all over him she wasn't too rapt. Always saw things in black and blue, my Mum did — especially Dad.'

'CUT!' shouts Glen MacArthy in caps. 'Your time has expired. Now, get out!'

And as we are leaving — 'By the way, you were shit'ouse as Claudius in Bill Gaskill's *Hamlet* at the Opera House in 1982.'

Later, at the Sportspersons' Bar, Cullen thinks of other ways to research a journalist — how about writing a short story and flogging it off to a publisher? You never know, they might buy it. 'A glass of milk, please, Judy?'

The barperson turns, she is in her fifties, reddened hair and well-turned ankles. Her eyes

— as big as saucers — are green as she guides them in the direction of Cullen at the bar's end.

'Sean?' she says with a warm smile. But, when closer, her expression changes to cover some embarrassment and disappointment. 'Oh ... '

'Did you think I was someone else?'

'Sean Scully, the actor,' says Judy with a sigh, 'you sounded just like him, but you're nothing like him at all. He's much taller and always reminds me of a wonderful journalist who used to drink here ... '

'Do you mean there is another actor around who looks just like Sean Gavelkind?' asks Cullen feebly.

'Gravelpit!' sputters Judy the barperson with consonant empathises. 'That mongrel? Christ, no! YOU look like HIM.' And back to business, 'What'll you have?'

'A kind word, perhaps?'

'Bastard! You ARE Sean Gavelkind!'

The magic is working.

STEPHEN MUECKE

MORE URBAN POSTMODERN TRIBES

'My *whole* persona is totally *Thirty Something*' — Jojo couldn't help seeing himself as a media product ever since he was head-hunted by Moynahan & Co. 'I work right up until two or three every night, just getting the cheques written and little things like that. My four hours sleep is as restful for me as Frances' eight to ten. She works differently to me. She's more a people person.

When Cath does the galleries on Saturday she always takes along her Brazilian friend Joachim whom she met at the Landsdowne Hotel last year. He's a writer and Pop theorist with a major success in glossy journalism.

'I like the way he makes things complicated,' she says.

Whenever her Pitjantjatjara 'family' come to town, Portia takes them to see Western movies or they watch Clint Eastwood videos at home. Portia met them when she had her initiation back in '89.

'They taught me how to fish, dig for yams and made a *wiltja* out of corrugated iron.'

'I've always been a bit straight, you know, but my parents are old rockers, you know, they have tatts and leather jackets that date back to *then*. We've taken to going over the Watson's Bay for fish and chips and a beer on Saturday afternoons. What's really good is that they're teaching me fragmentary thought and irony. I'm really loosening up.'

'Ever since Jean Baudrillard's visit in '84 I've been working on my Cultural Studies MA: "The

Discursive Construction of the Gum Tree". Judith Wright can be quite vicious on it, DH Lawrence was terrified, and forget Patrick White. You know what Baudrillard said to me? "The eucalyptus forest is almost gossamer ..."'

The Bondi intellectuals were all secretly relieved not to have to go to the beach because of the pollution. Now that the water's clearing up, Ann tells me that her reasons for not going now are 'purely structuralist'.

Down at Lorne in mid-summer Bruce reflects on the good old days when New Year's Eve saw the free-for-all with the cops. Even Hare Krishnas would join in.

Knowing the risks of being overcome by this morbid nostalgia, he sits up and lets his gaze wander along the beach in a process of tender discrimination: Silicon implants or not? He finds this reassuring.

After coffee at Northbridge we usually take the heelers down to Dog Beach for a poo and a play around. Nothing much happens really. At sunset it's really quite Zen.

Noel arrived back in Newcastle in time for the earthquake. Reports from the epicentre were coming in thick and fast. Fred had to pull over the Toyota thinking that the slight shift sideways was evidence of a flat. The radio was running laid-back vox-pop accounts of mild acts of heroism on the part of bank clerks and facts like 'some girls cried'.

SHANE MALONEY

THE OTHER CHEEK

The sheer volume of publicity generated by
Helen Garner's examination of the so-called
Ormond College Affair, *The First Stone*, has had
many repercussions. Not least of these is the fact
that another recent work on the subject of power
and sexuality in higher education had been
totally overlooked in the media coverage of the
issues. I refer to my own book, *The Other Cheek*,
which deals with the so-called Broadmeadows
TAFE Affair in which the buttock of a Hospitality
Studies student was pinched with a pair of
barbecue tongs during an end-of-semester
sausage sizzle.

The parallels between the two cases are striking. In both instances, young women found
themselves confronting the assumptions of en-

The young women I have called Stacey and Tracey, their alleged harasser Merv the Perv. trenched privilege. In both instances, powerful men were brought low, although it was only in the Broadmeadows Affair that this took the form of the kneecapping of the college's senior portion control instructor by members of the Blue Psychos Motorcycle Club.

As in *The First Stone*, the actual facts remain elusive. Perhaps no one will ever know what really transpired that fateful night at the sausage sizzle. Perhaps no one perspective is capable of encompassing the whole truth. That is why in writing *The Other Cheek* I decided to use fictional names to mask the true identity of those involved. As I see it, they were not mere participants in an uninvited bum-pinching incident, but the protagonists in an epic drama that throws into stark relief the issues of gender and power relations within the entire hospitality training industry and, by inference, society as a whole.

The young women I have called Stacey and Tracey, their alleged harasser Merv the Perv. Unlike the victims of Ormond College, all participants in the incident agreed to speak frankly to me and to put their version of the events on the record. Here, in this extract from *The Other Cheek*, is their story in their own words.

That is why in writing *The Other Cheek* I decided to use fictional names to mask the true identity of those involved.

Stacey: *I couldn't believe it when it first happened. There I was, queuing up for some coleslaw and a slice of buttered bread, when Merv the Perv sort of brushed against me. I thought he was just reaching for the sliced beetroot, but the next thing I knew he was nipping at my bottom with a pair of tongs. You can imagine my surprise. I nearly stabbed him in the thigh with a plastic fork, but I realised that I'd need his signature on the nomination form if ever I decided to go for Apprentice of the Year, so I didn't. Besides which, I had a fully-loaded paper plate in each hand and you know how delicate things can be to manage when you're in that sort of situation. So I just told him to piss off.*

It was only later, when I noticed that the tongs had left beetroot stains on my new white jeans, that I decided to take the matter to a higher authority. So I went to the Sausage Sizzle Organising Committee and said I wanted Merv the Perv to apologise and replace the jeans, or at least pay for cleaning the dirty pair. Well, all they did was reckon that Merv was just mucking around. Then they made some really off jokes about beetroot stains and irritable females. That's when I started to get really annoyed.

Merv the Perv: *I really was just mucking around, fair dinkum. Besides which, none of the other sheilas ever complained.*

Tracey: *Merv the Perv was a figure of authority. He had his own office and everything. So when he waved a sausage at me across the quadrangle, I was really traumatised. He said he was just offering me a bite, but I reckon he knew exactly what he was doing. From then on, as far as I was concerned, he was riding for a fall.*

Merv the Perv: *What's the matter with girls these days? Can't they take a joke? Besides which, all I was doing was shaking a bit of sauce off my sausage. You'd have to have a pretty dirty mind to make anything of that.*

Stacey: *After the Sausage Sizzle Organising Committee had given me and Tracey the brush off, I realised if we wanted satisfaction we'd have to take our complaints elsewhere. That's when we had a quiet word with Toula's big brother's friend, Turbo. He rides*

Now everybody feels sorry for him. And they reckon we're a couple of proper bitches.

with the Blue Psychos. They're a pretty rough lot to look at, the Psychos. Even the Vietnam Vets Motorcycle Club are terrified of them. But they've got this really strong code of honour and you know you can rely on them.

Tracey: *We didn't mean for them to actually do anything, just sort of put the wind up Merv the Perv, warn him off.*

Merv the Perv: *I told them. I said, look fellers, it's all been a misunderstanding. It's that cask wine. You know how it is. Ten or twelve glasses and a man can't be held responsible. Everyone knows that.*

Stacey: *Some blokes are just no good at reading the signals. Trying to talk his way out of it was Merv the Perv's big mistake. If only he'd had the sense to say he was sorry. Maybe then they wouldn't have stripped him naked and run over his legs with a Harley Davidson. Now everybody feels sorry for him. And they reckon we're a couple of proper bitches.*

Tracey: *Yeah, look what happened to us. Nobody cares what the whole thing has done to our reputations. This woman rang us up once. Reckoned she was a writer. Said she wanted to put our point of view and everything. She was going to ride her bicycle out and interview us.*

Stacey: *But then she found out how far it is to Broadmeadows, and we never heard from her again.*

Tracey: *Discrimination, really.*

Stacey: *That's what I reckon. Lucky we're used to it, eh?*

BARRY DICKINS

PARANOID TAXI

I can only call the shots as I see them. I can only get through each day the best way I know how. I used to be a happy boy. I liked and admired the fizzy tingly thing happy citizens call life.

But all that has changed since I got my taxi licence in Melbourne. I'm paranoid now, and see customers as murderers. Backpackers and harlots, even innocent children are lethal weapons in the wrong hands of the law — not that there's any law. We just make it up as we roll along. Roll with the punches the public throw at you. I live with my hundred and eleven great old father, Mike. He used to kill people for a living. Yes, he was a professional murderer. An assassin, Mike was. He smothered all my brothers with pillows as soon as they turned twenty-one years of age. He throttled our mother with his bare hands all those years ago — they hated one another. She was only forty and I miss having a gentle, guiding force in my life. I really do. I think her name was Grace. We are ruled by fear, no doubt of it, now that Premier Jeff Kennett is in charge of our lives.

What with his casino-culture and insane demands, like the prompt closure of municipal libraries, the downgrading of public lavatories and outer space observatories, the closure of tadpole ponds. Gee, when he started to walk around Melbourne personally closing down tadpole ponds so the little city waifs couldn't even scoop up a tiny little taddie, I knew our lives — indeed our whole social fabric — were over. We live in a siege-mentality-state in Melbourne. I arise at 4.15 am to put my ancient father in his high chair to give him his breakfast of Uncle Toby's Rolled Oats. I always joke with him as I put his bib on because it frightens him, the bib, for some reason.

He tries to gag in it and it's also hard to scoop the mucky porridge into his mouth, as he hates it. Christ, he hates porridge, but the doctors swear by it and it has to go in him to keep him keeping on. It goes everywhere, the oats. All down his front. In his opaque blind eyes. In his toupée. I have to rinse that out properly under the tap in the sink so he looks respectable later when we go for a refreshing stroll down to the two dollar shopping centre, where nobody has any money, as the casino-culture has robbed them all of their wages, savings, pride, sense of well-being, sense of humour and any possible future.

We marched together last Anzac Day, even though Dad's mates are a bit slow and are all dead.

He served in the Boer War and was mentioned in dispatches by some obscure Pom Colonel or other for conspicuous gallantry. That's a long time ago. See! Now look what he's done!

He just threw his Milky Boy milk bottle at me. I always call his milk bottle Milky Boy to get some sustenance down him.

I try to keep his teats clean but sometimes soldier ants arrive in them so Dad cops a mouthful of insects with his first morning feed.

Now I have to pick up after him.

Milky Boy bottle has gone all over our only posh item, an imitation nylon Turkish rug from Fosseys. See if I can get some tinned pear into him before I do the taxi.

Ah, no use. He's dead. Asleep or dead. It's the same thing under the present Government.

I pop him into his cot.

Out like a light. Tongue hanging out like a dead dog. Good on you, Dad.

Look, you're so skinny. I can't feed you up. You're fasting yourself out of the Victorian Liberal Party, aren't you, Dad.

Christ, I love the old bastard.

I'll put an extra pillow under him —
Maybe it should go over him.
Smother the old Reactionary.
Put him out of his torment.
I should shave him before I go.

Ah, his beard stopped growing a long time
ago. When snail-killer fell on it in 1930. He
worked for a time as a landscape gardener for
John Wren, Melbourne's leading criminal. Dad
was a kind of consultant and general-all-purpose
mate of his.

Ah, it's cold. I'll whack the extra jacket on.
Already got one under it. Pull the hood on. Put
me boots on and locate the car keys. Dad's
always playing with them. Stop playing with me
car keys will ya please, Dad.

Look at all the slobber on 'em!
I'll wipe it off with his pyjamas.
What a hopeless baby he's become!
Now, off.
Get the squeegee onto the frost.
Put the heater on. Ah, it doesn't work.
Sold it last week for a feed.

It's like being in the Great Depression years
again. I notice the local butcher flogs all the offal
cuts of yesteryear.

Bone marrow, bunnies.

Ox-tails. People are broke.

You never get a smile in our shopping centre, I
tell you.

Look at that old couple getting stuck into a
bottle of beer.

It's only early. Not even five in the morning.

Poor bastards! Lost their dignity.

You'd never see that in the old days.

Just trudging there on the footpath.

With a frosty plastic gar-bag for a hat. There go
the police.

Snot was freezing into long columns of
agony from both of my nostrils. I couldn't
help thinking I'd be better off dead.

Eating Big Macs
at this hour.

Look how lazy and fat they are.

Why don't they chuck the old people standing
in the rain a crumb of their Big Mac Quarter-
Pounder with chips and gravy?

And they're sipping coffee.

I can smell the revolting stuff from my taxi.
Wish I could afford percolated coffee. I drink a
new form of tea in the morning. You burn toast
jet-black then drop it in boiling water.

Dad loves it that way. Tears come into his eyes
when I put tea in him through Milky Boy, his
favourite milk bottle for poor babies who are
frightened to live out or die.

Now, what's this? I've killed someone.

Shit a brick, how did I do that?

I heard a loud bump-noise.

Better get out of the car and check it out.

No, it's only a woman. No, I'm seeing things. It's a dog. Nothing left of him

Come on boy, off the road.

Now his tail's come off. It's all maggoty.

Look at the disease all through him.

Shove him down the drain.

Like the memory of the dignity of the working-class.

Now let's try and get some runs on the board. No more buggerising around.

How about a job? The computer's packed up.

What did I do that computer course for?

I'll pull into Bourke Street Rank.

Look how depressed everyone is.

I've just about had Melbourne.

I've got $39 in the savings account.

My chequebook overdraft is well over the limit.

Look, to tell you the truth, I don't know how I'm going to get through this week.

I'm flat broke. Kaput!

Now, there's absolutely stuff-all at this dead rank. Computer is down.

Everything is down. I'm hungry, not just for a customer. I never had any breakfast.

Me guts are gnawing for want of appropriate sustenance. If I do okay today I'll eat out tonight.

The old man doesn't know what day it is. He can have two Milky boys tonight if I get in late.

Should put him on a drip. Put Victoria on a drip. I'll go on one too if I don't get a go soon. Do I need a break!

I'll get on the South-Eastern Freeway.

Hope I don't run out of gas.

Isn't it lonely out this way.

Nothing but depressed fellow motorists and a few frozen cows looking on. Without really thinking of the emotional consequences I fiddled with and opened my wallet, which had ants all through it.

'Sons of bitches!' I cursed, turning immediately into an American.

Too much TV with the old man.

I'm seventy-six years old; nearly a pensioner; almost as ancient as the old man. Nobody's quite that old.

I simply had to get some folding-stuff.

There was nothing in the fridge for my dinner. A block of Cadbury's nut-milk-chocolate, from memory; and some toast from yesterday is brunch.

I pulled in at the Hotel Burvale and hunted about for a pick-up.

It was freezing at the hotel taxi-rank and my knees were shaking.

Snot was freezing into long columns of agony from both of my nostrils. I couldn't help thinking I'd be better off dead.

I coughed and noticed spots of not very red blood all over my hankie. Well, it wasn't mine actually; one of Dad's.

Frantically I tried to get my heater going but the blow job out of it was actually refreshing. The night outside was positively South Pole.

I expected Sir Doug Mawson to hop in the back. 'One and a Husky to Base Camp,' I could hear him barking to me.

Inside the pub the last young blokes were having a chuck and the old sheila was standing up the glasses, swearing.

A cleaner came out and bit me for a light for his smoke. I abused him.

Give him language he hadn't heard for a while. Then a couple of dudes hailed me and I cheered right up. They looked pretty drunken, but I would've gladly given Satan a ride around the block for a few bucks. One was very tall, the other was as well, I noticed.

'Box Hill, mate,' the one who got in last said.

They started drinking.

Well, as long as they didn't screw.

I hate that. 'What part of Box Hill, mate?' I asked.

'Just Box Hill.'

I didn't like that, either.

They were going to be deliberately vague.

Hard to get on with.

The meter packed up. I couldn't believe it.

It jammed on 0.80 cents, even though its a $3.10 FLAGFALL.

For a moment there I thought of putting my Essendon footy hat over it.

'What's wrong with your meter,' one of them yodelled.

'It's stuck,' I said.

'We'll fix ya when we get there,' he answered.

All night saw me mucking around with them.

Up this forsaken sidestreet.

Up this other one. I had been on the road an hour with them.

They'd drunk all they had in their grog tuckerbag and for the past half-hour or so had been smoking marijuana. My eyes were watering.

Plus, to make matters worse they offered to pay me the fare to Box Hill in Buddha sticks.

'I don't smoke dope,' said I.

'Get out here,' said the one with one eye.

I apprehensively pulled up in Forty Street.

I thought it said footy. Never heard of Footy Street before. There was nothing there when I pulled up. Just a paddock. A paddock with a funny doorframe in it. No door or nothing. No house or anything. Just this bizarre doorframe. Like a doorway to my death, that's how I saw it.

'What are you waiting for?' one of 'em said.

'You got any bags?' I said, only I knew they didn't.

I was frightened.

He walked over to it but they then walked next-door to a home, a real brick place. With windows and heating. 'What a stroke of luck!' I cried out jubilantly.

I whirled my neck around to check my car was still there, as for the last couple of moments I'd only heard the one set of boot steps in the sloshy mud.

It was. Ah, what a relief.

It started to pound with torrential rain.

Absolutely it was deafening.

When we went into this second venue I noticed the one-eye-guy dead-latch the door. That dismayed me. He smiled.

They sipped their white wine sort of thoughtfully, as if they were intellectual or something.
They both stared hard at me.
For over two hours.

They then went straight to the fridge and got out lots of wine, beer and stuff.

'Would you like a steak, mate?' said the one with two eyes.

I couldn't talk. They didn't put on the heater so we just sat at this dirty rotten table, heaped up with cold wine bottles, dishes of butts, packets of smokes and mouse dags.

'I better get going, gents,' I said, trying to brave it out.

'Have a can,' said one eye.

'I don't drink, hate it.'

I had it and was sick up all down my front — like my poor father.

They sipped their white wine sort of thoughtfully, as if they were intellectual or something.

They both stared hard at me.

For over two hours.

'Why don't you put some music on?' I suggested. I felt like crying.

One of them replied, 'I don't know any music. Do you know any music, Tommy?' the other guy laughed and showed me a plastic wallet-thing full of various knives.

'Which one do you like?' he said.

'They're all nice,' I said. 'It's so hard to choose.'

My oxygen was sealed off. I couldn't breathe.

They started carving swastikas into a cheese board that was all greasy.

A phone rang and one-eye pulled it out of its socket.

He started trimming his fingernails with a boning knife; smiling kindly at me and sort of winking.

'I've got to get home,' I said.

'But you haven't had a drink or a smoke yet. Haven't you got any manners?' said normal-eyed one.

'Didn't your mummy teach you to smoke dope?' said his mate.

I ran without thinking and leapt straight through the dining room plate-glass window.

I laughed uncontrollably en route to the car.

The blood — all my blood —

I'm alive, I'm still here — the blood, all my beautiful plasma — it danced to my temple.

I drove home ecstatic.

I drove the wrong way, the wrong side of the South-Eastern Freeway back home to Dad.

He was starving when I got in and crying because he'd soiled himself.

'I will look after little man,' I blubbered and put a size 16 Huggies nappy round his arse.

I fed him in his high chair and put him to bed next to me all night long. He's not in any record book. But he's well over one hundred.

I just cried deep in him all night long.

I've never been so frightened in my life. Thank God I don't like marijuana.

I might turn out like those guys.

CATHERINE JENNINGS

ON GOLDEN BILLABONG

Hello, my name is Dulcie 'Snow' Dunder, and I live at the On Golden Billabong retirement home for faded Australian celebrities.

They're all in here; Ray Martin, Brian Henderson, Rolf Harris — ooh, he could wobble my board any day. I was always one for a beard. Till I started growing one. Poor Rolf's in the 'babies' ward now. On his pillerslips he does lightning finger sketches of the nurses ... and they used to think it was brown crayon he was using!

Remember Johnny Young? Kind soul. Went round the wards singing 'The Candy Man' and giving the oldies little bottles of lemonade and bags of lollies. Then two of the diabetics died suddenly, so they stopped him.

Who's that hobbling up the v'randah? Me pork pies aren't too good these days ... let's see, they've got a mass of spaghetti on their head ... oh no that's curls ... oh of course! It's Diana Bliss. The blonde leading the Bond. Somehow Bondy and Richard Court got a franchise on the bedpans. Now you have to put two bucks in 'em before the top slides back ... like that, see! Sorry, didn't mean to sling mud. Once upon a time I wouldn't have said boo to a goose. Except Richard Court.

There goes Bob Hawke, and wot-sername? Blanched Hazelnuts. With Linda and Hoges. Must be card night, those fellas are crib experts.

udy Davis is in Academy ward. Brian Brown's still n Rachel Ward.

Martha Gardiner's gone to that big woolwash in the sky. Dropped off the twig in her knitting circle. Sharing needles.

Maggie Tabberer had a nasty accident in the recent heatwave. Tripped over her long gold chains and lay flat on her back in the blazing sun for two hours until they found her, burnt black! They thought it was Kamahl until they cut her caftan off.

Elle McPherson's in D ward, poor lamb. Tucked up forever in the crisp white centrefolds of heavy duty hospital linen. Still, Sonia McMahon designed the hospital gowns so the nice long legs still get a guernsey. Jackie Love's gone bandy. Looks like a human wishbone.

Nicole Kidman came in after Tom took his final cruise. She went ga-ga. Started streaking. I hate it when she streaks. Her walking frame makes such a racket.

Judy Davis is in Academy A ward. Brian Brown's still in Rachel Ward. Angry Anderson was trying to get into my bloomers, but no way. He drops too much antacid. Last I saw of him, Dannii and Kylie were playing noughts and crosses in lippy on his bald head. Kylie married Jimeon you know, and became Kylie O'Reilly. Dannii teamed up with Boy George — O Dannii Boy ...

I caught the bouquet at Jana Wendt's funeral, and saw Dr Kevorkian, Unplugged, on 'Rage' that same week. So now I'm planning my final exit. Might get Daryl Somers to do the eulogy. He went religious, you know. Mormon. Still hosting 'Hey Hey It's Latterday'. Molly can DJ. P'raps Shirley'll sing his revamped biggie, 'All My Friends Are Getting Buried'.

In case you're wondering how come I'm here with all these famous old buggers, well, that was my bellybutton on the 'What No Potato?' billboards. The Hips That Launched A Thousand Chips. A spud on a torso. I'm a legend in A A — Advertising Anonymity. I was the mummy swathed in Kresta Verticals. So I've been a tummy and a mummy. I've worn so many fruitsuits I deserve the Hollywood Bowl. As a method actor, before a shoot, I eat big mobs of whatever I'm playing. It was a trial in that prune cozzy but I got the job done. Several times.

Well, must dash. My agent just faxed a voice-over script to Matron's office.

'Supp-Hose Support Condoms, for jigglers and danglers. Now available in tantalising flavours, especially for seniors: Mock Chicken, Cheese'n'Gherkin and Devonshire Tease.' Urrgh. That reminds me of a naughty joke. What's pink and wrinkled and hangs out Grandpa's 'jamas? Grandma! Hoo-roo!

CLINTON WALKER

TRAGEDY: THE PERFECT DESIGNER DRUG

Have you heard about the latest new designer drug? It's called Tragedy. Ecstasy is out, in case you didn't know. The drug that kills with kindness is now as passé as pierced goatees. Today it's time for action, time to look out for Number One — because, you know, people are all the same in the end, they just wanna screw you — and Tragedy is the ticket.

Tragedy is scenes. Tragedy is hysterical bullshit. Tragedy is about getting absolutely unnecessary, about so indulging yourself, from a zenith of narcissism to a nadir of nihilism, that nothing else even enters your field of vision.

You will find yourself in strange, dark, crowded places in the middle of the night, entranced by music even more banal than last year's, and you're so tragic you can't even come out and be tragic about it. On 'tradge', you don't take a trip, you trip over.

So how did I find out about Tragedy? I suppose, as so many drugs do, it found me first. I was sitting in my local hoteliery, which is kind of like a cross between the Karova Milk Bar and the Ettamogah Pub, when this bloke sidled up to me. I knew he was a drug dealer because he was wearing one of those old 'Choose Life' T-shirts. It's not as if I looked like some young drug-hungry maniac. I probably looked like an old drug-hungry maniac. He sold me a couple of caps.

It was expensive. That always makes a drug more desirable. Sixty bucks for a black capsule containing a few grains of black powder. It looked like nothing I'd ever seen before ...

Tradge. Scientific name — methyldramaque-enamphetamineoverload. Derived from melted down old Depeche Mode records. These records aren't that easy to come by these days, existing largely in the back of collections from whence they're too embarrassed to emerge. This decidedly non-virgin vinyl is combusted (again) and the resultant thick sticky black substance is combined with patchouli oil and VB and cooked until all the liquid evaporates. What's left, in crystalline form, is Tragedy. Simply mix with a drink, preferably VB, and stand back.

If you could OD on Tragedy — which, unfortunately, you can't — an antidote would be another new, very rare drug, made by a similar chemical process, called ME262. Stumbled upon by a couple of renegade chemistry students in an inner-city sharehouse, ME262 is made from incredibly rare old Radio Birdman records. One black and red cap can set you back up to $200. The boon is, where tradge gets you feeling sorry for yourself, ME262 allows you to project the blame! Two down, only ten steps to go to meet David Crosby in the big detox in the sky.

Tragedy hasn't quite reached epidemic proportions yet — it hasn't even reached trendy levels — but it's catching on. It is, after all, the perfect drug for the moment. People have had enough of caring and sharing, their fill of the milk of human kindness. It can only go sour.

Says Pamela (not her real name), 19, a riot grrrl and new convert to Tragedy: 'My boyfriend — well, actually, he's my ex-boyfriend now — he's a skateboard shaper and we used to be really cool together, but then I found out he was going out rollerblading — rollerblading! — with this other woman, and he was still sending me e-mails all the time, so I just had to do something.' (Pamela will eventually kick and move up the coast.)

Tragedy does away with the need for anyone else. It's complete self-possession. It doesn't matter if anyone else has something to say because you won't hear them anyway.

The key to Tragedy, my research shows, is that it actually doesn't do anything at all. Has no net effect whatsoever on the body or the brain. This makes it the perfect drug as it's not addictive physically and has no negative side-effects. And it's precisely because Tragedy is a drug that does nothing — what researchers call the Clayton's Syndrome — that it's becoming so popular.

Critics say it's because users feel ripped-off, but that's missing the point, in that a big part of the tragedy experience is just that — feeling ripped off. Anyone can feel hard done by occasionally, but everyone wants a bigger problem than the next guy. And in Tragedy you can dig your own grave.

Someone on tradge is pretty easy to pick. They're the people who always look determinedly desperate. They will suffer any amount of insults and indignities, like door bitches and dogs, to wallow in the social primordial slime that is a nightclub. They'll be rubbernecking terribly and clicking their tongues and rolling their eyes, because for them it never quite gets there — and that's the final beauty of Tragedy. It's unsatisfying.

So you are going to want more, and that's where the dealer comes in again. For him, it's a pretty good racket, because Tragedy's not yet illegal. But police will be swooping upon it with all their usual aplomb.

'Our informants inform us that young people are in fact taking drugs,' said a police officer who refused to either be identified or sell me anything. 'We believe that the 1980s comic strip character Garfield the Cat has become a cult symbol of this kind of activity, and we will be concentrating all our efforts in this area, wherever we see him.'

Me? I wasn't sold on the stuff. Maybe I am just burnt out, but I went home, and like a junkie looking for a stash he's sure he hasn't lost, I turned the house upside down looking for a Tracy Chapman record with which to dampen down the creeping sensation I felt. I was only thankful the next morning that my taste's not so bad as to own such a hideous thing. Besides, I got through the night anyway. I did, however, I have to admit, ease the pain with a few Traci Lords videos.

They say there's no hangover to Tragedy, but I know better. People get up like normal people, in at least a reasonable, businesslike frame of mind — if not positively sunny — and go off to their jobs as systems analysts or personal trainers, or to their media studies classes. Now that's ugly.

The next time I saw that dealer man from my barstool mountain, I got up and went over to the jukebox and punched in K8 three times. I sat down again at the bar and ordered another gin and tonic as the opening strains of some

Smashing Pumpkins song I hated rent the smoky atmosphere. I've found that sort of thing, in threes, is usually the best way to deal with such situations. It was as if nothing was changing. The dealer skulked off in search of easier quarry.

DORINDA C HAFNER

GOTCHA — A DAY IN THE LIFE OF SHOPPING

It's hot. It's sticky. It is Adelaide, an usually dry city. And it is summer. I'm irritable. The kids have been running around and screaming all day. It's three o'clock in the afternoon and it's Saturday. The shops would be full of people and I hate Saturday grocery shopping. 'Mum, when are we going shopping?' 'Mum, can we go shopping?' 'Mum, you promised!' The kids, James, four, and Nuala, three, were restless. We did not have a pool and the paddling pool we did have was now too small. There are only so many games that one could keep playing on a hot day and we did not encourage them to watch too much television, so I had been racking my brains for something to do with them other than story-telling or reading.

'Yeah, talking of shopping, you haven't spent all that money, have you, on groceries? Surely foodstuff cannot have such a high-mark up? What's the world coming to?' Now it's their father's turn to whinge — the biggest kid of them all. Bingo! 'I'll take him shopping so he has that wonderful experience of shopping with kids on a hot day in a supermarket.

We all piled into the car to go shopping at Coles Supermarket at Parkholme.

Of late the children had developed a habit of demanding lollies and sweets cunningly left around the checkout counter to entice children to indulge in exactly this behaviour, so I was secretly glad of their father's help on this occasion. To expedite matters I suggested we take two trolleys, he with the kids in one down one aisle and me with an empty trolley down another aisle. We agreed to meet back at the checkout when we had honoured our respective shopping lists.

Julian, their father, a slim fair Englishman, was wearing matching grey and red shorts and T-shirt bought from a local department store and the kids were also in shorts and identical T-shirts. They took off for aisle three and I took off for aisle five. I whizzed round in twenty minutes flat grabbing the detergent, grabbing the tea, grabbing the fly spray, grabbing the peas, grabbing the bath soap and grabbing the cheese and there I was, laden and ready to cash up. I turned down aisle two and there was Julian, his back to me, comparing the product labels. I could hear the kids but could only catch a glimpse of their clothes. On the spur of the moment I decided to lighten things up a bit and surprise him. I left my trolley alone and crept up behind him. I put my arms right round his hips and spontaneously grabbed his balls and shouted 'Gotcha!' He turned around and with a face etched with absolute surprise the man said, 'Oh, do we know each other?' 'Oh, I'm so very sorry! My most humble apologies,' I said, releasing his balls.

At times like this, no amount of apology can release you from the predicament. In fact, the more you try to explain, the worse it gets, and all I could say was 'I ... I ... I ... thought you were my husband.' The man's surprise deepened as he looked into my African face. At least if I could go crimson red it would help express how mortified I felt. I could tell he didn't believe me. He had obviously assumed my husband would also be African and therefore my tale was most unlikely.

I retreated speedily to my trolley feeling as though I had been hit with an anvil on the back of my head. I whizzed round towards the checkout, hopefully in flight towards the supportive arms of my family. My troubles were apparently not over.

I found my real husband trying to explain to our children why they should not have lollies from the checkout counter. I must have looked exasperated

Oh, I'm so very sorry! My most humble apologies,' I said, releasing his balls.

because he said 'What's the matter? Are you all right?' Before I could explain, I saw my daughter throw a tantrum because she was not allowed to have a lolly. Spontaneously, and without thinking, I joined her in a tantrum — stomping my feet, jumping up and down and flailing my arms about. 'I can't stand it! I can't stand it! This is parental abuse! Get me out of there!' It must have lasted all of twenty seconds, but when I finally stopped, I noticed my children staring at me, my real husband staring at me, the man whose balls I clutched staring at me and all the other shoppers staring at me with pity in their eyes. Everything was quiet in the shop except for the humming of the fridges. As my eyes scanned their faces a thought occurred to me. Well, at least the man will see that I wasn't lying. He and my husband were wearing identical clothes and, strange as it may seem, so were our children.

My children took my hands reassuringly. Their father put his arm around me and whispered, 'Take the kids, let them help you into the car and wait for me. I shall join you shortly.' My kids led me to the car. I did not utter one more word until we got home. But the good thing about all this was that the children never threw another tantrum at the supermarket checkout. In fact, whenever we went shopping from then on, they offered to stay in the car whilst I did the shopping.

COODABEEN CHAMPIONS

REBIRTH OF AUSTRALIAN CRICKET

Richo: Next caller; go ahead please, you're talking to Tony.

Caller: Gooday, Tone!

Tony: Who's this?

Caller: It's Don here, Tone!

Tony: Oh, g'day, Don, how are you? Where are you calling from, Don?

Don: I'm ringin' in from Devonport.

Tony: Oh good, Don.

Don: I want you to help me ... Have I got a good question for you? You know the commentators over the last couple of days?

Tony: Mmm ...

Don: At various times, Tony, they've said it's the rebirth of Australian cricket.

Tony: Yes.

Don: Well! How can you have that with all these old blokes? You have to have young blokes in the side to get a rebirth!

Tony: Yes, well, actually that is a good ... err ... that one I can answer ... It's just that the spirit of Australian cricket has been born again; ergo, a rebirth. And this is the first time, Don, that ...

Don: What's ergo? Keep it simple for us down here in Tassie.

Tony: Well you never know who is listening. People might be tuned into us thinking it is Radio Helicon which is on ABC National at the moment which is very highbrow.

Don: I heard one of the commentators talking about that today.

Tony: What's that?

Don: They said that that that that innings by Jones yesterday ...

Tony: Oh yeah.

Don: Yeah, it brought back memories of the helicon days of Bradman.

Tony: Well, there you go.

Don: Is that what Radio Helicon is all about?

Tony: Yes, well not quite but ...

Don: Old cricketers and great scores?

Tony: Exactly, Don; but the rebirth of Australian Cricket ... It's just a figure of speech, Don.

Don: Well, I want to run these past you, Tony.

Tony: Right, fire away.

Don: Now, is it the rebirth? Or have they just simply laid the foundation? Or is it a resurgence? Or are we in fact on the threshold of a new era? Or are we just going through a rebuilding phase which has begun to bear fruit? They have had a go at all of 'em, Tone! Which one is it?

Tony: I think it's a little bit of all of those expressions, Don.

Don: Fair dinkum. Why don't they just say they are back in town?

Tony: Well, talking about 'back in town', what about Dean Jones and England.

Don: Hey?

Tony: What about Deano possibly going to England?

Don: Deano Jones? Oh he would 'ave to, wouldn't he?

Tony: Oh, I think so.

Don: One of the commentators said today said, he said 'he has written his own ticket'. Have they got a travel agent there or something when the players come in after they have made 200, they just write out their name on a ticket?

Tony: Well, no. No, it doesn't mean that, Don, but ...

Don: One of the others said the same thing.

When Bevan took his fifth wicket, he said ... 'he can write his ticket to England'.

Tony: ... mmm.

Don: What does the team manager do? Doesn't he write that stuff out?

Tony: Look, look, look, Don. Look, they are just figures of speech.

Don: Unbelievable, mate,

Tony: Is the message that you are trying to get across is for the ABC commentators to keep it simple?

Don: Yeah. Keep it simple for us down here in Tassie, Tony.

STEVE BEDWELL

STILL MORE BITS AND PIECES

THE SHORT-PITCHED DELIVERY

The short-pitched delivery is difficult to play.

You must rock onto the back foot.

You must get over the short-pitched delivery and keep it down.

You must never take your eye off the short-pitched delivery.

My coach told me this as he sat with me in the ambulance.

THE FLOOD

The flood came through my lounge room.

The flood destroyed my one-month-old hi-fi VCR and 68 centimetre flat-screen colour television with surround sound and Teletext.

The flood soaked my new three-piece leather lounge suite with matching ottoman.

The flood washed away my stereo with 5-disc CD stacker and twin Dolby cassette decks.

Actually, the flood barely wet my carpet, but what the insurance company doesn't know won't hurt them.

THE DUNLOP AQUAJET

The Dunlop Aquajet was an excellent tyre.

The Dunlop Aquajet exhibited superb roadholding qualities under all conditions.

My father's Valiant Charger had Dunlop Aquajets fitted as standard equipment.

With a Stanley knife and some white paint the Dunlop Aquajet can be made into a decorative tyre swan.

TIM GOODING

ELVIS PRESLEY HAS LEFT THE CATHEDRAL

It was hot, but Elvis drew the line at wearing shorts. The locals wore them everywhere. They would no doubt wear them to church, but for Elvis, shorts were the point where dignity overrode fear of discovery. He thought he MIGHT have agreed to wear short pants in *Blue Hawaii*, but that was a long time ago. He could not be sure. Neither his memory nor his knees were what they once were. And in those days he did what he was told, but NOT ANY MORE. Now, he was free and the chocolate-coloured safari suit with long pants seemed the ideal solution. It was cool, roomy, and commonplace. He selected a yellow shirt with short sleeves and floral motif in two stripes down the front, such as he had seen worn by taxi drivers in Manila, and white shoes with a flap that folded over the instep and a small fake buckle at the side. The shoes were a size too big. Elvis had no socks. The complete outfit cost six dollars and fifty cents. He combed his hair sidewards, in the changing-room mirror. The left-hand corner of his top lip rose. He smiled. He didn't look like Elvis any more. NOT EVEN with his lip curled. He left his old clothes in the changing-room and walked out of the Opportunity Shop into the sunlight of Oxford Street.

Emerging from Clancy's Food Barn with a pizza sub, he was almost knocked over by a shopping trolley.

The dry-cleaning tag scratched at the back of his neck. He appeared to wrestle with himself, struggling with both hands to remove the tag while curling his toes in an attempt to gain traction inside his shoes. The velcro under one of the fake buckles gave way. His foot burst through the flap. He stumbled, scraped his toe knuckles along the hot footpath, hopped in a circle, fell against a white four-wheel-drive, and stared down as dark blood appeared under the nails of the shoeless foot. He often stared at his feet these days. They had hardened since he left Graceland.

Changed colour, taking on patches of yellow and blue which seemed to respond to the weather. The nails were cloudy and thick. In need of cutting. Difficult to reach. The nail on his little toe was black and reminded him of Priscilla. She had worn black nail polish, at some stage, back then.

He hobbled back to rescue his shoe from a small child with dreadlocks, a Rasta T-shirt, and no pants. He did not look the child in the eye. it had not yet been born when the King was pronounced dead, but Elvis was taking no chances. The King was part of race memory. Even seed-of-smoke-brained-gene-bent-basket-weaving-white-middle-class-weekend-Paddington -Rasta race memory. Elvis did not approve of sub-cults. Or their T-shirts. Or their bare-assed children. There were so many sub-cults these days. All characterised by one thing: they were UGLY. Would style ever return? It was dangerous for him to look at people. Surrounded by ugliness, he felt less regret at spending the rest of his days staring at his feet. Stepping onto the road, he forgot they drove on the left in this country, and was almost run down.

Emerging from Clancy's Food Barn with a pizza sub, he was almost knocked over by a shopping trolley. Priscilla pouted at him from the illuminated cinema poster on a bus shelter. Touched-up and body-doubled, but definitely Priscilla. Arching in the arms of Leslie Neilsen.

Leslie Neilsen?! Elvis wished Priscilla well, but deep in his heart he knew she shouldn't act. Leslie Neilsen?! Elvis rolled his eyes. He had seen *Naked Gun 2¹/₂* four times. He was thinking of seeing it again when the trolley crashed into the back of his heel and the semi-naked child with the Stussy hat toppled forward into the dozen free-range eggs. Both Elvis' feet bled as he quickly left the scene of the accident.

His days were now full of the strange musty quiet of charity shops, and the shining ugliness outside. Close calls with foreign traffic. Dirty semi-naked children. Blotchy hard skin and slow-healing wounds. The avoidance of eye contact. The avoidance of cameras. This above all. The most photographed man in history. He was early. He waited in the park opposite St Mary's, listening to the soothing click of lawn bowls during lulls in the traffic.

He was awoken by the smell. A man was sitting beside him. Something sour rose low in his throat. He held his breath and turned away, letting the scent of summer grass calm the churning in his stomach. The man sat closer than was usual for strangers. His hip touched Elvis' ribs. This had happened before in a park in London, and by the river in Paris. Then, Elvis panicked and ran. Now he feigned sleep, knowing the attraction was not him but his clothes. If this man, the others, knew Elvis' face, the significance eluded them. They stopped because they recognised the clothes. Saw the absence of socks.

Three more. Two men. A woman who looked like a man. They stared, heads jutted, before approaching. Slowly, at an angle, pausing en route to reconfirm. Afraid. They no longer trusted their senses. The attempt at discreet approach was betrayed by a twitch. A flailing arm. A sudden jerk of a head. They bumped into each other. Threw haymakers. Shouted like angry dogs. Elvis nuzzled the grass and waited. One pulled out a bottle in a crumpled brown paper bag. The others smiled and patted their friend. They sat. They would stay quiet until one became greedy. While they sat beside him, Elvis knew, the rest of the world would stay away. The notion that he too might smell tormented Elvis.

He thought there was something earthbound about St Mary's. Serviceable, but not uplifting. Perhaps it had been built by socialists. It did not float in light, soar, take his heart with it, like Chartres. It was not bravura like Milan. Nor fraught with piety like Santiago de Compostella. It did not compare with Constantinople or Jerusalem or Mexico. Elvis smiled. He had become a cathedral snob. The squat ochre of St Mary's reminded him of a stack of shortbread, fretted by mice. The tops of the stumpy towers flanking the main portal had been nibbled right off. The bells rang for six o'clock.

He hovered in the gardens at the side while the summery crowd talked their way slowly up the front steps. A young woman hurried along the path towards him, tying a scarf over her hair. Elvis stepped into the garden bed and pulled the rotten blooms from a pink camellia bush. He had observed that people took little notice of gardeners. Upon passing, the woman stopped. Elvis submerged his face deep in the heart of the bush. He reached for a far bloom. Sidelong, through leaves, he saw her turn to look as she finished knotting her scarf. His heart beat hard. His body melded further with the camellia. He saw her look away. She took out lipstick and held a small mirror up to her face. Elvis glimpsed a slash of red lips, and as the mirror tilted, the woman's eye. It seemed to catch his. He was inside the camellia bush. About to run. The woman rolled her lips together, jammed on the top of her lipstick and strode around the corner.

He slipped into an empty pew behind the congregation, near a side exit, under the flat gaze of Our Mother of Perpetual Succour. He thought of his own mother, Grace, in a pastoral landscape with four blue rivers issuing from a fountain. Vernon was there, walking with her in the garden, emanating love. With infinite patience they waited to be reunited with Elvis, and Jesse, who died unbaptised and would be released from Limbo on Judgement Day. What would Jesse look like? Would he still be a baby? Elvis imagined a line of nappies hanging in Heaven. The pew in front creaked as he lowered himself, slowly, to pray. His knees clicked. The kneeling board groaned. Breath stalled in his throat. The congregation continued praying, heads bowed. Elvis prayed. He resisted a feeling that the flock had yielded to temptation, and was turning round to sneak a look.

They opened their hymn books as Elvis hauled himself to his feet. He wanted to sit. He remembered a recording made late in his career, while seated. In a spirit of atonement, in this place of forgiveness, he stood. Eyes closed, he sang. He sang, and felt his spirit rise. He sang and felt his soul freed. He sang and was washed clean. No longer Elvis. A boy from Tupelo who could sing. One by one the congregation heard, stopped, turned to look. Elvis left the cathedral, knowing he could not return.

HUGH LUNN

TAKING A BATH AT WIMBLEDON

Winning tennis matches at Wimbledon is nowhere near as easy as it looks on television. I was beaten there myself in 1980.

Not being a seeded player, I was, of course, relegated to an outside court, Court 9: but still just a long lob from the famous Centre Court.

This was a good omen. Court 9 — one of fifteen Wimbledon tournament grass courts — is known in tennis circles as 'the graveyard court', because of the number of top players surprisingly beaten there.

Not that I was favoured to pull off an unexpected victory. My opponent, with several Wimbledon titles under his belt, was more fancied. But let's just say a lot of English people were impressed that I was from the same

Australian state that had produced such greats as Roy Emerson, Rod Laver, and Wally Lewis.

Some thought my age, thirty-nine, against me because even Ken Rosewall had not been able to overcome the passing of the years. But I wasn't worried.

As I tugged sweatbands on and checked the gut strings in my graphite, polyurethane foam, tensilium, fibreglass-reinforced racquet I pondered the Wimbledon singles victory of Britain's Arthur Gore when he was forty-one years old.

Yes, I had done the research for my first match at Wimbledon.

I even pulled a ruler from my bulging tennis bag to measure the length of the emerald-green grass on the court, just to make sure I was playing on a level field. Yes, it was three-sixteenths of an inch long at both ends: exactly the length Wimbledon grass is mown to daily during the tournament.

The grass was lush with a soft, oily leaf — which is why it wears so quickly during the tournament. But on the first few days, when there is a new surface of untrampled grass, the ball skids off so fast that champions can easily fall to big servers. 'On the first two days a swinging serve will put you out on Church Road,' my coach whispered: and I let fly with a series of expletives to get into Wimbledon mode.

After all, this was disconcerting news. The serves at Wimbledon mightn't look that fast on TV, but the two-and-a-half-inch yellow ball has been electronically timed there at over one hundred and fifty miles per hour.

And here I was suffering jet lag from the twenty-six-hour flight from Brisbane.

Still, I stepped forward confidently for my first match on the sacred Wimbledon turf. I looked up at the ivy-covered stadium towering above the court — a concrete monolith that gave the world forever the phrase 'Centre Court', and which took a direct hit from a German bomb in World War II.

The clock set in among the ivy on the wall signalled the start of play: 2.00 pm.

Above the ivy was the scoreboard which registers every point played inside the Centre Court stadium, so that the thousands milling around outside know the score. Those outside even clap this scoreboard when a Centre Court match is close. Rod Laver once told me the reason we tennis players love Wimbledon so much is that it is the only place in the world where you get clapped twice for the same shot: first inside, and then — as the score goes up — outside.

It was great to be among champions.

I looked across at Court 8 next door and there was British Number One, Sue Barker, clubbing the ball much harder than I could.

She was even more stunning in the flesh.

I was glad now that I had taken advantage of the facilities in Wimbledon's well-stocked dressing shed, which provides free hair oil and several tortoiseshell hair brushes: the reason Edberg and Agassi always look so good.

I looked across at Court 8 next door and there was British Number One, Sue Barker, clubbing the ball much harder than I could.

The dressing shed even featured recessed lighting, green carpet, weighing scales, and a gold Rolex clock. I was particularly pleased with the silver shoehorns because they had long handles: after a tough match I guessed I might have some trouble bending down to get my shoes on.

This was, of course, the exclusive dressing shed for top players only. Most of the 128 male entrants for Wimbledon each year are required to dress elsewhere, in less opulence.

Outside, the sign said it all: 'Gentlemen's Dressing Room'. Inside, there were six large green bathtubs — and a couple of attendants to run the baths. 'Which bath would you like after your match, sir,' one of them asked. 'The Bjorn Borg or the John McEnroe?' He said the Borg bath would be shallow and cold with a sponge, and the McEnroe hot, deep, with a stiff nail scrubber.

I ordered the McEnroe.

Up some stairs, past the players' entrance to the Centre Court where there is an inscription in gold lettering from Rudyard Kipling's poem 'If': 'If you can meet with triumph and disaster and treat those two impostors just the same.'

It was a quote I bore in mind as our umpire climbed into his high chair and announced the phrase that is heard only at Wimbledon: 'Play shall be continuous.'

The umpire was Jimmy Moore, once a Brisbane lad and now official referee for the annual tournament at Queens Club in London. My opponent was another former Brisbane tennis player, Ken Fletcher, a Wimbledon doubles champion who is a member of The All England Club, Wimbledon.

'You know,' said Jimmy, as we tossed for serve, 'It's a pity you weren't here two months ago. We had a great Wimbledon tournament this year.'

GREG MACAINSH

PAR AVION

It was a wet, windy, dismal Melbourne Sunday night in mid-1978. Jane and her sister Louise had just finished watching 'Countdown', Dragon's 'Are You Old Enough' (the week's number one song) was playing as the credits rolled into another dull evening of television. 'Fuck this, Jane, I'm so bored,' Louise groaned from the bean-bag in front of the Phillips 21 inch. 'Let's go out.'

'Lou, we've been out every night since Thursday, I've got to work in the morning and I'm buggered.' Jane headed for the toilet ... too many cups of Lan Choo. 'Where do you want to go?'

'The Underground,' stated Louise, applying her mascara at the mirror while Jane pulled up her jeans and stabbed the button on the Caroma.

'That place is full of fuckwits and Macedonian wankers,' hissed Jane. Her double bed and a night reading Cleo ever inviting.

'Well, are you coming or not?' quizzed Louise, Jag denim jacket buttoned up to the neck, ready for a cold hundred-yard walk down to Domain Road to hail a Silvertop.

'Okay, but I don't know what for, and I'm not staying out late ... shit, have you seen my keys?'

'Come on ... yeah, they're by the phone.'

In the back seat of the cab, Louise smoked an Alpine. Jane extrapolated to herself how disgusting she was going to feel after eight hours on her feet at the Myer cosmetic counter tomorrow.

They split the fare, a two dollar note apiece. Mandy the door bitch greeted them. 'Guess who's having dinner in the VIP lounge?'

'Jesus Christ and Sonia McMahon,' snapped Louise, undoing her jacket and adjusting her halter-neck top.

'No, David Lansom, his manager and some people from Deliberate Records.' Mandy knew what Lou's agenda was and predicted her persona was about to do a U-turn into Miss Sociability.

'Really?' inquired Jane. Maybe her prognosis of the night was about to become obsolete.

There was nothing like an English rock celebrity to transform an uneventful weekend into a vista of possibility.

Ron, the bouncer who stood guarding the

roped-off entrance to the lounge, let them straight through.

'Bacardi and coke for me and vodka and lime for Lou,' Jane ordered the bar girl.

Looking around the room she soon spotted Lansom and his entourage. Surveying the debris on their table it looked like they had been there for several hours. The meal was long gone and champagne and cigarettes seemed to be the main indulgence.

The girls settled on stools at the bar, adjusted their minis and tried to appear disinterested in their main objective.

'I can't fucking believe he's here,' breathed Louise, finishing her drink in two swallows. 'He's a lot shorter than I thought he'd be.'

'But still gorgeous,' Jane added, her mind a million light years away from the Yardley counter on a Monday morning.

'Good evening, ladies.' It was Gary, the promotions manager with Deliberate, coming towards them, glass of Krug in one hand, bottle in the other.

'Hi, Gary, where have you been?' said Lou, her whole being animated and totally willing to forget Gary's drunken groping at her boob tube at the last record reception they were at.

'Showing David round town. This was the last date on the tour and they go back to the UK tomorrow morning.'

'Come and meet everyone.'

Gary led them to the table.

'Excuse me, everybody, this is Louise and Jane.' Gary didn't bother introducing anyone at the table by name to them. Deliberate Records staff weren't hired for their social etiquette. It was more their ability to supply influential radio programmers with copious amounts of drugs and sex that got them the job.

'Sit down, ladies,' beckoned a swarthy gentleman in a brown velvet Saville Row suit.

Jane couldn't stop staring at Lansom. He was deep in conversation with a woman who had publicist stamped all over her heavily made-up, hair sprayed, Channel Nine appearance.

'I'm Simon Bellgold, David's manager,' Mr Brown Suit said, pouring the girls a glass of Krug each.

'We're celebrating the end of our tour — did you see the show?'

'Er, no, we couldn't afford tickets,' said Jane. It was actually true. They had discussed going but a recent shopping splurge at Mr Figgins had left them dangerously close to being short for rent this month. Subsequently they were a no-show for David Lansom's Plastic Caravan World Tour.

'Pity, if you'd called me I could have got you front row and backstage passes.' Bellgold topped up the girls' glasses.

'Yes, I'll keep that in mind for next time, Patti.'

David Lansom rose from the table and farewelled his publicist as she kissed him on the cheek. Patti wobbled towards the club's exit and Lansom finally cast his attention in the direction of the girls. Jane made sure she caught his eye. He smiled and headed over to where she was sitting.

'I'm David Lansom, it's a pleasure to meet you.'

'I'm Jane and this is my sister Louise.' She suddenly felt awkward in the presence of such a famous and cultured Englishman.

'I see you've met Simon, the secret of my success,' smiled Lansom. 'Come, sit down and talk to me.'

Jane moved to fill Patti's recently vacated chair.

Lansom was wearing a black velvet suit with black satin lapels and a white turtleneck shirt. His blonde hair was impeccably coiffed and Jane knew his watch was probably a Cartier. She'd seen something similar in the Vogue magazine she read on the tram going down St Kilda Road on the way to work.

'So, you live here in Melbourne?' asked Lansom. 'Yes, but I want to go to London and work there for a couple of years. Just to check the place out,' responded Jane. She was starting to relax. The champagne was kicking in. He was so much more attractive in real life, she thought. Not as effeminate as his publicity photos. She became vaguely aware that the rest of the people at the table had their attention on her and Lansom but she tried to ignore that distraction.

She did notice however that Louise appeared charmed and humoured by Mr Bellgold. Not her type — too old, thought Jane. However, Louise was animated and appeared to be explaining to him the nuances of Australian slang. She could hear words like 'sheila', 'dunny door', 'root', being bandied around. 'How crass,' thought Jane. She never considered her sister had much in the style department.

Lansom told her that London was a great place but he was finding his inspiration in other parts of Europe. He explained to her his penchant for Flemish painting and how he kept an apartment in the artists' quarter in Berlin.

Bellgold kept the champagne flowing. A change from the usual Drops on the Rocks the girls normally drank at clubs. As David Lansom spoke, Jane found herself inventing a new future. One in which she was the confidante and lover of this exciting and enigmatic man. Her life would be a blur of parties and receptions. They would be photographed together at exotic and glamourous locations all over the world. His next album would be dedicated to and inspired by her. She felt herself grow more and more open to him as she finished her fourth drink.

'Well, my lad, what say we adjourn to the B&B.' It was Bellgold, panatella in hand and arm around a very tipsy Louise. 'The car's waiting.'

'Yes, I think so,' replied Lansom and turning to Jane, asked, 'Would you care to accompany me back to our hotel?'

Jane and Louise's eyes met for a moment. Louise had that 'I'm going anyway' look.

'Why not,' said Jane as they walked to the front door. It was pouring rain as they got into the limousine.

The two couples were sitting opposite each other in the back of the car. Bellgold had his right hand kneading the flesh between Louise's halter-neck and miniskirt. Louise was nestling herself into his tubby frame. David Lansom sat a respectful distance from Jane but placed his hand on top of hers in an almost paternal manner. The first physical contact between them.

No one spoke during the short drive to the Hilton. In the lobby Louise turned and whispered to Jane.

'He wants to take me to London.'

'Oh sure,' hissed Jane.

As they stepped from the lift on the eighth floor, Bellgold turned to David. 'Lou and I are just going to my room for a moment — we'll join you later.'

'Fine, Simon,' smiled Lansom.

She had never been into a room at the Hilton and certainly not a suite the dimensions of this one. Lansom was on the phone ordering more champagne. A bottle of Bollinger arrived promptly.

'We'll be more comfortable in here,' Lansom ushered her into the master bedroom.

Jane sat on the edge of the king-size bed, sipping slowly. The champagne was fine but if she drank **H**is tongue found hers and his hands moved straight to the clip on her bra. too quickly the room was likely to start rotating and she didn't want to miss out on this experience of being alone with Lansom by passing out, or worse still, vomiting. That had happened once or twice.

'I'd like to kiss you,' she heard him say as he sat down beside her. She put her glass down on the floor.

Not hearing or sensing any resistance, he leaned forward and as their lips met she stifled a gaseous burp. His tongue found hers and his hands moved straight to the clip on her bra. His intensity surprised her. No longer the polite and charming host, his animal instinct was now firmly in charge.

Slipping off her halter-neck with one hand and her bra with the other, she was unsheathed and naked under him in what seemed like a matter of seconds. His tongue traced the circumference of her breasts and his fingers probed her moistness. The effect of the champagne diminished abruptly and her senses became fully aware. She found his hardness and guided him in. Their coupling was furious, thrashing, hammering. It went on for longer than Jane had experienced with any man before. With the few Australian men she had slept with, it all seemed to be over in a matter of minutes. Different positions, from the bed to the floor, to the sofa, the coffee table and back to the bed. Sweat poured off them. Finally he came. She felt the rigidity subside and the Englishman return. Holding her close he whispered, 'That was wonderful.' 'Yes,' she murmured.

'*N*ow I've got something to remember you by,' he grinned.

He kissed her while his hand stroked the small of her back. His mouth engulfed her right earlobe, his tongue wet and vacuuming. She felt something different. In an instant she realised her diamond stud earring had gone. The clip must have come loose. 'Damn.' She felt it being pressed against her cheek by his tongue and went to retrieve it.

He swallowed! It was gone!

'I can't believe you did that. Why?' Jane hissed. He was weird, all this manic sex and now swallowing her earring.

'Now I've got something to remember you by,' he grinned.

They shared a cigarette and Lansom made her coffee. She sensed he wanted her to go. Jane felt reality come rushing back. She realised he wasn't going to invite her to stay and the Myer Lonsdale Street employees' entrance started to pervade her consciousness.

'Well, I better be off then.'

'Sure, I shall call you a cab,' said Lansom, eager to facilitate her departure.

'Don't worry, there will be plenty in front of the hotel.'

'Can I have your address and number? — I'll get Simon to send you an itinerary and some contact numbers if you get to London.'

Jane wrote her name and address on a piece of hotel stationery and got dressed. They kissed and Lansom led her to the door of the suite. 'Thank you very much. Melbourne will never be the same.' he smiled. 'Take care.'

She stepped into the long corridor. Having no idea where Louise was she took the lift to the lobby and climbed into a Black cab.

Back at the flat it was silent. Louise wasn't home. 'Bitch,' thought Jane. 'Maybe he is going to take her with him.' She removed what was left of her make-up. The clock radio glowed 2:19 as she pulled the doona over her. Sleep came swiftly

Knightsbridge, landing at JFK to begin American tours or being photographed leaving the Chanel boutique in Beverly Hills. The alarm rang at 7.00 am. Louise still hadn't returned and Jane boarded the tram to Bourke Street and to work.

The hangover didn't release its grip until she returned to the flat that evening. Louise was lying in bed, having been thrown out of the Hilton way past checkout time.

'I think I'm in love,' she groaned.

'Bullshit,' yelled Jane from the kitchen. 'Do you want a cup of tea?

'He's sending me the details of when I can go to meet him,' said Louise, lighting a Kool.

'I'll believe that when I see it,' Jane retorted putting the mug on the bedside table. 'We've had our fun and now it's back to dreary old life in Melbourne.'

She was right. The next couple of weeks were like any other. It rained, the sun made a brief bid for glory and then the grey clouds returned. Work, supermarket, laundromat and a pub or disco on the weekend. Jane had even gone dancing at the Underground with a couple of girls from work and not remembered the Deliberate Records party.

One Wednesday afternoon, after a non-eventful day demonstrating foundation make-up to the acned faces of wagging schoolgirls, Jane collected the mail from the letterbox downstairs.

There was an SEC bill, some junk, and a blue envelope with a Par Avion sticker and four United Kingdom stamps on it.

The thought rushed through her mind that it was for Louise. 'Shit, if that bitch gets to England before me I'll scream.'

No, the letter was addressed to her — Miss Jane Brown. The handwriting was beautiful, copperplate bordering on calligraphy and definitely not written with a biro.

Resisting the urge to desecrate the envelope by ripping it open immediately, she hurried up the stairs, got a knife from the kitchen drawer and slit it carefully open. Inside was a note written in the same immaculate script on stationery from the London Savoy. Jane's heart-rate soared and her knees were shaking as she read.

> *Dear Jane,*
>
> *Thankyou for the wonderful evening in Melbourne. I just wanted to return this to you. Don't be alarmed — Simon always carries latex gloves. He says he wears them when he counts all the filthy lucre. I use them for other purposes.*
>
> > *Fond regards,*
> > *David Lansom.*

Pinned to the bottom of the page was a tiny package. Louise opened it and out fell a small ball of tissue paper. She unfolded it and there was her earring — the one Lansom had ingested.

The chuckle started in her chest and raced up to her throat. It became a full-blown laugh and then a series of hysterical shrieks.

'Oh my God!' A million thoughts raced through her mind. When? Where? How? But mostly, why?

The chuckle started in her chest and raced up to her throat. It became a full-blown laugh and then a series of hysterical shrieks. She rocked back and forward on the kitchen chair.

'What the fuck are you so happy about,' yelled Louise, coming in through the still open front door and plonking four Safeway bags down on the laminex table.

'Any mail for me?'

Through the kitchen window Jane noticed the fading afternoon sun make an instantaneous final appearance before disappearing behind the ever-present cumulonimbus. In that moment Melbourne seemed like a magical place and her life a remarkable adventure.

She felt the laughter settle to a quiet smile and find its own permanent place in her psyche.

'No, nothing for you. Just a bill.'

'Damn, he said he'd write.'

STREPHYN MAPPIN

SOUTHERN EPIPHANY

Quite some time back, in the early not-so-politically-correct seventies, I was a member of a club called The West Coast Divers. Now, to call it a diving club was probably being a little generous, when, in fact, the sole reason for the club's existence was to kill fish.

Every weekend, weather permitting, fifteen of us would clamber into four or five shabby boats and tear out a couple of kilometres offshore to some hidden reef where we'd don wetsuits, masks and fins and take our pick of the local aquatic population. (This sort of recreational activity went out of favour in the late seventies and eighties, though it has enjoyed something of an upsurge recently due to the realisation that spearfishing is actually a lot more ecologically sound than most other forms of taking fish, but that's another point altogether.)

About once every two or three months, our club would take part in a spearfishing competition, usually at some desolate seaside town several hours from Perth. I never did well in these, simply because competition is not a particularly driving part of my nature. I took part for two reasons: firstly, I did not own a boat and it was the only way I could get out on a dive; secondly, it gave me a chance to see a bit of the country, albeit mostly from underwater.

This particular competition was to be held down south at Margaret River, a town which, at this stage of its history, was known mostly as a surfie hangout and refuge for people seeking an 'alternative' lifestyle.

After finishing lectures on Friday afternoon, I managed to cadge a lift from one of the club's seniors. As well as being the best diver in the club, Bob had a panel van, so he was a handy individual to cultivate. Since none of us could afford to stay in motels, and we were all too macho to own tents, anyone with a van was like the owner of a hotel on wheels. If you stayed in their good books, you had a chance of getting a spot to sleep.

Only three people had vans that weekend, so it was a rather crowded convoy that wound its way down the Albany Highway, towing battered boats packed with diving gear, stinking fish bags and a terrifying array of spearguns.

The only problem with Bob was that he was an avid fan of Abba, and any long trip with him was usually filled with hour after hour of 'Fernando' or 'Mama Mia' played as loudly as the van's tape deck would allow. My theory was that he did this to put everyone in the club out-of-sorts in order that he do better in the competition the next day.

Apart from myself, the rest of the club worked in various trades, and were usually exhausted by Friday nights. And except for the driver, everyone tried to get a bit of sleep, which was an especially difficult task if you were having to contend with four Swedes singing at the tops of their voices about lost love, distant guns and potato farming.

We arrived in Margaret River just before ten that evening, with just enough time to nip into the pub for a cold one or twenty before crashing out for the night. Even though we had to be up at five in the morning for the competition, most of the divers would have a drink if there was a pub within an hour's drive of where we were staying. (I joined them once, but after vomiting through my snorkel the next day while still five metres underwater, vowed I'd never do it again.)

While they drank, I curled up in the back of the van and slept, confident that since I was first to be asleep in the back I'd have a possie for the rest of the night.

Since I'd been spending a lot of late nights studying, I was in an especially deep sleep, so it was something of a shock to find myself briefly airborne, then to have the air knocked out of me as I hit the ground. It was even more shocking to see four drunken, full-grown men giggling hysterically as they clambered over the top of me into the back of the van and slammed the tailgate, leaving me thrashing about amongst the dirt and leaves in total darkness.

The gate swung suddenly open again, bringing on the interior light in the van. Bob popped his head out, grinning wildly.

'Juniors get to sleep outside,' he slurred, just before slamming it shut once again.

'Fuck! Fuck! Fuck!' I heard from somewhere off to my left, from which I gathered that I wasn't the only junior destined to spend a freezing night in the open.

In all, three of us had been tossed out into the cold, one from each van; all of us the most junior members of the club. Naturally none of us was overjoyed. I received some drunken condemnation from the other two, who were convinced that since I was the teetotalling student everyone had been joking about in the pub, it was my fault they were out here with me.

'And to cap it off,' Mario breathed beerily in my direction, 'Ralph is on the prowl.'

This was not good news.

Ralph was the bête noire of Margaret River. An ex-bikie, he'd taken a rather bad fall sometime in the late sixties, losing one leg. Since that time, he'd managed to wangle himself a job as one of the council rangers, and had become an object of terror to the hordes of surfies (and occasional divers) who move in and out of town depending on the state of the ocean swells.

There were tales of Ralph discovering illegally camped surfies down various bush tracks and of him attacking them and their vans with a baseball bat. For a guy with such a chequered past, Ralph was a stickler for people obeying the Margaret River camping rules.

He would cruise the secondary roads surrounding the town late at night, his spotlight always at the ready, striking terror into the hearts of all who dared to try and sleep outside the designated areas.

People said that, since his accident, Ralph had developed an almost evangelical fervour for upholding council laws.

Another rumour had it that Ralph also grew the best dope on the South Coast, and that the baseball bat was simply his way of making sure he always had enough product to sell come harvest time.

Once our eyes had adjusted to the darkness, we were able to work out just where the vans had parked. We were in the trees off one side of a firebreak trail which ran along the back of the Margaret River Cemetery. The club had successfully parked their vans here once before, working on the principle that people, especially rangers, do not spend a lot of time visiting cemeteries in the dead of night.

Now, Margaret River is not a warm place at the best of times, and towards the end of winter it's positively Arctic. The three of us were hopping from foot to foot, breath clouding the air, slapping ourselves violently to try and keep warm. Repeated hammering on the sides of the vans had first been met by laughter and then snoring. We were not going to get any sympathy from the club seniors. And since we only had the clothes we were standing in, we were in for a very cold night, and there wasn't a lot we could do to remedy the situation.

Ralph was the bête noire of Margaret River. An ex-bikie, he'd taken a rather bad fall sometime in the late sixties, losing one leg.

Until, that is, I had a stroke of inspiration.

'I don't know about you guys,' I chattered

out, 'but I'm putting on my wetsuit.'

With a rush, we invaded the boats where the diving gear had been stored.

Everyone who had ever spent an evening illegally camped around Margaret River knew the sound of Ralph's souped-up council ute.

A full diving wetsuit is a wonderful thing. Made of lightweight neoprene, it covers a diver from the top of his head down, leaving only his face, hands and feet free. Dive boots then cover the feet, gloves the hands and a mask goes across your face, but we decided to do without the latter for sleeping. The combination works along the lines of a pressure cooker, storing the diver's body heat so that it builds up inside the suit.

Once we had struggled into the suits — which is not an easy thing to do in the darkness — we took a stack of old hessian fish bags and made our way through to where we could bed down for the rest of the night.

Naturally, grave sites are the best for this, and we chose three in the oldest section of the cemetery, deciding there was little chance of us stumbling into a freshly dug plot around there. I can remember thinking it funny at the time that three guys who would quite happily punch a three metre shark on the end of its snout if it was trying to eat their catch were in abject terror of falling into a hole in the ground, but then different things terrify different people.

After checking as best we could for bull ant nests, we laid down our fish bags and curled up for the evening.

I was woken by the sound of a powerful engine switching off. Somehow I'd incorporated the noise of it arriving into whatever dream I was having, but the silence when it stopped jerked me into full awareness. I could feel the sound of the engine still hanging in the night air, and I knew immediately who had arrived at our sleeping spot.

Everyone who had ever spent an evening illegally camped around Margaret River knew the sound of Ralph's souped-up council ute. He'd dropped a worked V8 into it, and it had a growl like a rabid dog.

The darkness was suddenly sliced open by a brilliant shaft of light which moved slowly across the cemetery grounds, stopping just above my head. There was no sound, only the heightened intensity of my breathing.

We're meat, I thought to myself, deciding whether to run for it then, leaving the other two sleeping divers to their fate, or to lie motionless on the off-chance that Ralph hadn't actually seen us.

The light never wavered, and after a few

terrifying minutes I began to smell the acrid odour of dope. Ralph was having a quiet joint in the comfort of his ute.

We looked like Thunderbirds on Thorazine.

If I lie quiet, I thought, he's going to finish up and drive on.

I twisted my head around to take a quick glance at Mario and Tim, who were still sound asleep, when I saw something that made my blood run cold. Just behind the grave sites where we were sleeping, lit dramatically by Ralph's spotlight, were half a dozen two metre high dope plants.

'Oh shit,' I murmured, which was all that was needed to make Tim wake up.

'Shit what?' he grumbled. Then he too became aware of the spotlight.

'It's Ralph,' I whispered. 'And we're smack bang in the middle of his plantation.'

'Plantation?' Tim's eyes became very, very wide.

'Dope plantation. It's right behind you.'

'I'm going to run for it,' he said. 'Make sure you go in another direction.'

'What about Mario?' I queried.

'Don't you worry about me,' came his reply from behind me. 'For starters, Ralph's only got one leg, so he can only come after one of us, I reckon. And I'm also running just as fast as you two.'

'On the count of three,' I whispered. 'One ... two ... THREE!'

And we all leapt to our feet.

Intense cold can do strange things to the human body, even if it is protected by a wetsuit. We'd probably been lying there a couple of hours before Ralph's arrival, and in that time the cold had crept up from the ground and wrapped itself tightly around our muscles.

The best any of us could do was stagger jerkily to our feet and waver in the startling glare of the spotlight. We looked like Thunderbirds on Thorazine.

'Oh Christ,' Mario moaned, 'I can't move.'

'We're dead,' hissed Tim.

I half-turned towards Ralph's ute, which, to my blinded vision, was like a vague squat shape topped by a brilliant, incriminating eye. It held me pinned, bug-like against the darkness behind.

And then there was just a long period of silence; the three of us, still with fish bags slung around our shoulders, lazily undulating to and fro in the light, with night insects like silent, frenzied Kamikazes hurtling into the glare from the top of the ute. The fug of Ralph's joint filled the air around us.

'What's he doing?' I finally whispered to the others.

'Polishing his baseball bat,' suggested Tim. 'I

wish I could get my legs to work.'

'Maybe he's asleep.' Mario sounded hopeful.

Nothing happened for another few seconds, even though I was certain Ralph was suddenly going to come hopping out of the driver's side door of the ute at any time, baseball bat at the ready.

'Perhaps if we back off really slowly, and make sure we don't do anything to startle him, he'll just let us go,' Tim said quietly.

'Nah, there's something wrong,' I replied, feeling the circulation slowly easing itself back into my limbs. 'What if he's had a heart attack?'

'Ralph hasn't got a heart to attack,' said Tim.

'RALPH,' I called, but because of the cold it came out more like 'RRRAAALLLPPPHHH!'

'What are you doing?' Mario whispered nervously.

Still nothing.

'Hey, Ralph, you there?'

As there was still no reply, and no sound of movement from Ralph's direction, I took a shaky step towards the ute, having to hold my arms out in front of me to keep my half-frozen legs balanced.

As I teetered in his direction, a sound suddenly filled the night air, a sound so chilling it froze me in my tracks. A small herd of goosebumps stampeded from the base of my neck, thundered down my back and went into hiding somewhere in the vicinity of my extremely puckered rectum.

It was the sound of something, some animal, either dying or suffering such pain that it was beyond any hope or reason.

The keening started quietly, but increased in a series of slow hiccuping bounds until it resonated through the thin, cold air.

'Mother of God,' Mario moaned, and slumped dramatically to the ground, muttering in Italian.

It was then I realised that the sound was coming from the ute.

I took another staggering step in Ralph's direction, holding my arms out placatingly. 'It's okay, Ralph,' I called out, but this was greeted by the roar of the mighty V8 coming to life and the suddenly spinning of the ute's wheels in the gravel of the graveyard.

A spray of small rocks whipped into my face as the ute reversed helter-skelter between the tombstones, clipping a couple in its haste, and crashed backwards through the fence. It spun a magnificent handbrake turn on the roadway and hurtled off through the trees in the direction of town, the spotlight flicking in and out of life as it disappeared into the darkness.

'What the ... ?' Tim started to say, then he burst out laughing. 'Can you imagine what we must look like?'

After spending the rest of the night huddled

beneath the boats — we abandoned the graveyard, thinking that Ralph might return with a shotgun or, even worse, a priest — none of the juniors did all that well in the competition, though overall our team did better than the opposition.

I returned to Perth tired and stinking of dead fish and returned to my studies. Sometimes, at meetings of the diving club, Mario, Tim and I would joke about the night in the graveyard; how we must have appeared rising from the ground all dressed in black with tattered hessian around our shoulders and our eyes glowing red in the spotlight. Tim would do impressions of me staggering forward with my arms outstretched, moaning 'Raaalllph' in his best ghostly voice. But after some months we grew tired of the story and it, and its possible effect on the demon Ralph, gradually disappeared from our repertoires.

It was several years before I returned to Margaret River, on this occasion to stay with some friends who had decided to move to the area. As I approached the town, moving down an avenue of brilliant golden wattle and happily reminiscing about the time four years ago when a trio of local Bronze Whalers had mistaken me for breakfast, a large sign caught my eye.

The sign was off to the side of the road, half-hidden by a spray of branches. An arrow indicated a rough gravel track through the trees and welcomed visitors to 'The Assembly for the Curious Visions of Christ'.

As my car moved past, more of the sign emerged, and from behind the spray of branches appeared an all-too-familiar painted face with the words, 'Worship Nightly With Brother Ralph'.

STEPHEN MUECKE

URBAN POSTMODERN TRIBES (COME AGAIN)

'Henry and I scarcely survived the stock market crash. All we had left was the MGA, a trip to Perisher and season tickets to the opera. Henry is working on how to rebuild our "cultural capital" and I'm pretty much into reading corporate biographies.'

Jay reviews porn movies for the gay press. 'For me, *Study in Stud* is a triple A rating — fine neo-classical imagery with some surprising dimensions. I applied the usual test and was changing gear all the way through, coming for the fourth time as the credits started to roll. Blue Heaven Studios, all I can say is "Ta".'

Wayne and Maria met when they started working at Westpac. They've been saving and are about to exchange contracts on a semi in Elsternwick. The wedding will be in the spring, that's if Maria doesn't get sick of Wayne's little joke: 'I want to make a small deposit,' he says. 'Regularly. For the future.'

Joan is Executive Officer for the Women Barristers Association, and edits their monthly journal, *Legs*.

'We run articles on things like affirmative discrimination and dealing with male subordinates. And some surprisingly useful phone numbers crop up in the Personals column.'

Our son Sam, according to the Psychiatric Unit of the Queen Elizabeth Hospital, suffers from 'Attention Deficit Disorder (ADD)'. This means that he doesn't listen in school.

As if by compensation, or encouragement, he was awarded the Principal's Achievement Certificate for 'Good Behaviour on an Excursion'. The only trouble was, he went on the wrong excursion.

Ann-Marie runs a kick-boxing studio called Divine Women. 'We think that mace and whistles and all that stuff is so tacky. You need to have confidence as well, otherwise you're going to just drop your bundle in an emergency. A girl's best assets are a good pair of thighs and nice hard callouses on the balls of the feet.'

In Rundle Street at the King Kong, Donny and Daisy appreciate a sauternes with *foie gras* for lunch. They open an excellent little cleanskin from the vineyards, and in drinking it they can't help quoting James Thurber once again: 'It's a little wine without much breeding, but I'm sure you'll be amused by its presumption.'

The Creative Writing Department went on a retreat to Mt Victoria. On the way up in the train they sniggered at the passenger reading *Pathways to Higher Consciousness*. They were reading the Saturday Review sections and wearing Penguin Classics T-shirts.

DAMIEN O'DOHERTY

ENGINEERS HAVE ROUGH BALLS

It was past midnight when we arrived at Sydney University for the Engineering Students Ball. Two thousand punters had paid forty dollars each for the privilege of consuming as much liquor as they could possibly handle. As we stepped over prone bodies, it was obvious that most had consumed more than they could possibly handle.

We were 'Jaguar', a sometimes funny comedy/singing act that parodied seventies rock duo 'Cheetah'. Clad in wigs and six-inch long false eyelashes and carrying costume-filled suitcases, we made our way to the back of the hall and down a staircase. We arrived in an ill-lit and somewhat deserted car park known as 'the band room'. This was good. Usually we changed and made up in a pub toilet where drunken girls in tight jeans would inevitably ask to borrow our mascara. A definite shortcut to an eye infection.

We put our bags down on the dirty floor and surveyed the room. A few seconds later a pale-skinned, black-clad figure emerged from the darkness and ventured toward us, and what appeared to be his fellow band members were soon visible wandering aimlessly in the background. They all bore the same stunned expression.

Zunny

Showuz Yertitz

'Don't go out there,' said Pale-skin, grabbing me by the shoulders and staring me hard in the face. His eyes were wide and glazed, his mouth trembling.

'Don't worry,' cried Jane, my best pal and other half of Jaguar. 'We've played some pretty rough gigs.' He gave her a glance, paused for a moment and then, like Lurch in the 'Addams Family', made a throaty shuddering sound before disappearing into the shadows. He was soon followed by his fellow heavy metallers. I can't remember their name ... Sharkfin or Destructo or something.

Deciding our messenger must be a bit of a wimp, Jane and I proceeded to squeeze ourselves into our multi-coloured bodysuits. We attached

beaded
waistbands — remi-
niscent of Bo Derek's 80s plaited
hairstyle — checked our woollen pubic hair
and clipped on pointy chain-bedecked bras — a
somewhat different look in a time when people
still thought Madonna was that woman in the
paintings holding baby Jesus.

Dressed and ready, we waited quietly. The
headline act was a band called the Sunny Boys.
We could hear the 'why are we waiting' style
chant from the crowd above. 'Zunnyboyoyoys!
Zunnyboyoyoys!'

Confident that they would be thrilled to the
back teeth when they caught sight of our little
outfit, we got our call and headed for the stage.
Our taped backing music filtered feebly through
the various conversations, chants and groans.
The air of expectancy was probably similar to
that experienced in the heady days of the
Colosseum. Rome ... not Vegas.

From the black gaffer-taped platform known as
the stage we looked out on a sea of what can only
be described as faces. I would love to say that there
was an accompanying hush as we took a hold of
the mike stands. But no! It was all Zunnyboyoyoys!
Showuz Yertitz and louder still — Get Orff! Quite
deafening for so early on in the proceedings.

Thinking we could win them over, we introduced ourselves and did some hilarious things with a plastic hand and a Flake bar. It was not long before the crowd began to throw themselves wholeheartedly into the audience participation segment of the show. Since there was no audience participation segment in our show, we found this a little disconcerting. Deciding to make a contribution to our small array of stage props, they began hurling plastic cups in our direction. Slowly at first, like tropical rain ... pitter ... patter ... glancing off a temple here, a forehead there. The crowd's generosity knew no bounds and soon we were being pelted. We retreated upstage and took some small comfort in the knowledge that we had out-manoeuvred our foe. The cups were now landing on our toes. They were plastic after all and could only travel a short distance.

Then some 'spark', who obviously had a real bent for engineering, decided they'd travel further if weighed down with something. The experiment worked and I was the first to get a beer shampoo. Jane looked smug. She had always been more adept in the ducking and weaving department, but her wig, like mine, was soon plastered to the side of her face, complete with lemon garnish. Frantically signalling the sound man to cue our backing tape we decided to power through the songs and forget about 'the comedy'.

As we were getting drenched, a roadie jumped onstage. Chivalry is not dead, methought. 'Don't damage the fuckin' equipment!' he barked, and swung a few punches crowdwards. As I watched his departure my eyes fell on a large, full jug of beer within easy reach. I was holding it in no time and thanked God for my 'manna from heaven'. Choosing a target wasn't difficult. Three of my assailants were in a congratulatory huddle and seemingly unaware of the impending missile. I took aim

... Clutching her tightly clad buttocks in a kind of arse-muppet way, she ventriloquised ... 'I can speak your language'.

and hurled. I don't know why, but as if by some freak of nature, like the Red Sea ... they parted, and the entire contents of my precious vessel landed all too well on some hapless and innocent-looking female. I stood gaping in horror, the empty jug dangling from my right hand.

Then something awful happened. What was generally referred to as Australian Champagne hit me square in the eyes. I recognised it immediately as a non-vintage aerated vinegar. It was young enough to pack a punch and it stung like crazy. Now I'd had enough. Enraged by temporary blindness, I flicked my sodden head and stamped my feet angrily. With an abrupt clockwise swivel that would make any Duntroon boy proud, I John-Inmaned it off the stage. Pausing atop a small stairway I motioned for Jane to join me in my exodus.

No such luck. If they were handing out prizes for wild monkey impersonations, Jane would have been a sure thing. Gyrating madly she threatened the crowd, 'You paid forty bucks for this and you're gunna get the whole show!'

What a trouper. There was a guy in the front row who could easily be used to promote the 'Yes' vote in a Boot Camp Referendum. My buddy turned her back on him, and clutching her tightly clad buttocks in a kind of arse-muppet way, she ventriloquised ... 'I can speak your language'. Now she was getting laughs. My heart filled with pride. This was the theatre! This was the meaning of 'the show must go on!' The energy fuelled by pride seemed to empower me. I was suddenly channelling all the greats of the entertainment world ... Garland, Midler, Tim (Tiny). I was probably channelling the failures as well, but their names didn't immediately spring to mind.

Untangling my eyelashes and taking a deep breath I prepared to go back on. Smiling confidently and raising my arms in a victorious, yet dignified manner, I calmly walked to the edge of

Gyrating madly she threatened the crowd, 'You paid forty bucks for this and you're going to get the whole show!' the stage and copped a full glass of beer in the middle.

Our little concert continued in much the same way, with me taking refuge in a drum kit and Jane sheltering behind a speaker box. The liquid applause died down somewhat and I kidded myself that the enemy were beginning to enjoy the show. The truth was they'd run out of ammo and were too drunk to queue at the bar for more.

We were quiet in the taxi on the way home. Both frail and in a state of shock. After a while Jane suggested quite seriously, that in the future we perform with raincoats and umbrellas. I told her to shut up. We got back to our hotel and sat motionless on the beds. We'd had all those drinks and come home sober. A cloud of misery hung over us. We stared into each others eyes and began to laugh. And laugh. And laugh. We laughed long and hard. I was curled up on the floor and couldn't see Jane through the tears, but I could hear her howling. The pain was intense. My only worry was that, being a cheap hotel, we had no phone for easy ambulance contact. But what a way to die!

I still think of that night and those engineering

students and the effect alcohol has on the brain. I think of it whenever I'm crossing a new bridge in a high wind, or taking a fast lift to the top of a shiny office tower or enjoying a wild ride at the Royal Agricultural Show. I wonder if they passed their exams and went on to do great things, and I wonder if they remember two young women who were paid to make them laugh.

Rick Kane

CAR AND I

I'm not car crazy. Never have been and all up and all down, I am probably never going to be. Trouble is, cars are so much a part of the everyday experience in a big city. Or in Perth, where I grew up. I want to tell you, for what it's worth, how a motor atheist can get caught in the glare of Australian culture's spotties.

I grew up in Belmont, a working class suburb of Perth in the 1970s. That's a double whammy when you don't have one iota of car-ness running through your veins. In Belmont, boys start talking about engines as they are being born. By the age of fourteen they know exactly what car they are going to marry. Being Belmont in the 70s, it was without question a Holden or a Ford (and one with more pistons than a human has fingers).

Remember (if you can), that back a couple of decades, as a populace, we didn't really give a flying fuck about the environment, let alone the effect of smog on our own fair city. Smog was something that LA had and man, did we crave it. So cars were big, the engine bigger. Down my end of town the boys lived and breathed doing up their cars. Carbon monoxide was their Tower of Babel. The car was not for commuting, it was for communicating. I didn't have much to say in those circles. I certainly didn't perk up and let 'em know about my first car, the one dad got me for a good three hundred bucks. It was a 1962 Ford Anglia. That little beauty got me the hell out of Belmont.

The Anglia got me across town to see bands like The Elks at The Subi, Warner at The Shents or whoever at Hernando's. Trouble was, the thing that set me free was the very thing I thought I was escaping — the car. I loved that little Anglia. I loved the $89 K-mart cassette player (that I had someone else install) a whole heap more. Come to think of it, I didn't love the car that much. When I lost my licence for drink-driving, the car just sat in my parents' front yard until a wrecker bought it for $50. I had moved out and on. It was a teenage love, I guess; one-sided and of the moment.

Even when I was driving it around, I paid it scant regard. And for that I, of course, paid the price. For many months there was something wrong with the radiator. Not being particularly handy or giving much of a hoot I would just make sure that the radiator was topped up. Most of the time, anyway. If it overheated I always had a plastic bottle of water in the back seat. Most of the time, anyway. The cassette player never failed, it was my true locomotion.

One glorious morning I was tootling along to college. If I said 'Born to Run' was playing some tangential metaphor could be created, but I would be spinning porkies. No, I was playing Joy Division's 'Love Will Tear Us Apart' full bore. I was in a hurry as I had a mid-semester Education tutorial test to sit. I crossed the Causeway and headed up Riverside Drive, Langley Park playing fields to my right and to my left, the Rottnest ferry departing the Barrack Street jetty on yet another vomit-inducing sea trip. Then under the Narrows Bridge. A bridge so aptly named and so illuminating of the city planner's lack of pre-science that it inspires the scratching of the head. Unless of course you have already seen the Barracks Arch facade. Then along Riverside Drive as it weaves deliciously around the base of Kings Park. Certainly one of the more beautiful roadways you could find yourself lost in.

At this point I notice the car is, well, starting to splutter and hiccup and cough and choke. Having a direct connection to the heart of the

Anglia, I figure that if I just slow down (a little) I will still get to Nedlands

It, in turn, dies, to be replaced by a Kingswood. Dad is finally happy — his son has become a man.

Teachers' College before the bastard car conks out on me. As with all mechanical decisions I make regarding the car, I am wrong. So very wrong that just as I take pressure off the accelerator the car stops dead on the road. It then allows me enough time to consider why I didn't have the radiator fixed a long time ago before it comes back to life to lurch forward five yards then jolt right back. Mmmm, whiplash to boot! Steam, as if from Hell's own geyser, turns the front bonnet into a smokescreen that Spinal Tap would proudly produce. Unfortunately for me I'm not in a rockumentary. I am running late for a test, with an excuse that ranks at the bottom of the food chain of excuses. I get out of the car (the one I love, remember, and pull the front seat forward to get my trusty bottle of water. I figure I'll have to wait five minutes or so before I can top up the radiator. My trusty bottle is waterless. It is without water. It is so empty that an ant could not wash itself all over with the last remaining drop. And so I am, as Steve Martin was in the car rental office scene from *Planes, Trains and*

Automobiles, fucked. I didn't swear or scream or even kick the car. In an exasperated tone, with my confidence fading like a stick-on tattoo, I said: 'Where the hell am I going to get water from around here?' I said this, oblivious of the imposing expanse of water that lay before me. I was standing on the bank of the Crawley Bay section of the Swan River. Geddit? The river is so big it has bays. It took me a while to do that lateral thinking thing that is so common these days. Even then, like a tool I wondered if river water might do damage to the radiator. Then I laughed. A paradoxical laugh that knows that situations such as this will not be uncommon to one such as me living the urban life.

To this day I still think of the whole Nissan Urvan thing as my parallel universe period.

And so we get older. The Anglia becomes a Datsun 180B. It, in turn, dies, to be replaced by a Kingswood. Dad is finally happy — his son has become a man. Driving an Australian icon is not nearly as neat an idea as you may imagine. The parts are cheap and easy to procure but that argument for choosing a car, like modernism, is destined for the museum. The Kingswood was far too rigidly Australian. So I ditched it and got a Nissan Urvan. To this day I still think of the whole Nissan Urvan thing as my parallel universe period. We all have a slab of our life that doesn't resemble any of the rest and this was mine. For two years I drove around in a seven foot long by seven foot high tin box. Apart from twenty-seven days when I used the Urvan for carrying equipment needed at school camps and the fourteen or so days when it was used as a removalist van, I don't think the bulk of that vehicle was needed for ANYTHING. I could never escape the incongruity of it. Every time I looked in the rear-vision mirror I was reminded of the depth and pointlessness of man's existence. How inextricably we are connected to our own destruction. One time a friend drove the Urvan around Kings Park while four of us went tripping off our heads in the back. That is the best use I ever made of that most mistaken purchase. How I arrived at the decision to buy an Urvan inverts and confounds Molyneux's famous theory.

Needless to note, I had not advanced my knowledge or desire of anything vehicular. Basic logic should have informed me to 'know thy enemy'. A bent for the sport of heuristics must, it would seem, make me rise to the challenge of understanding something as simple and beautiful as an engine. Nope. Not at all. I thought of car engines the way an amoeba thinks of, um, car engines. This lack of equilibrium in the relationship and my role in the imbalance would find me amerced again and again.

One tragic morning everything I had irreverently mocked about cars crystallised into a Frankl mirror from which I can never avert my gaze. It happened as follows: Hungover to shit I stepped out into the midday sun. The Urvan waited, silent, knowing the inevitability of this moment far too well. I climbed into the driver's seat. One of the pluses about Urvans is the position of the seating. It is about a foot higher than in an ordinary car. Under the centre seat is the engine. An Urvan has no front bonnet. This makes driving feel safer. But I digress. So I'm sitting in my Urvan and I turn the key. Nothing happens, the engine doesn't turn over, the van remains motionless. So I turn the key again. I do so ten or twenty times. With exactly the same result. This was as perplexing to me as waking up in the morning, attempting to get up and not being able to move your legs. I'm stumped. I considered my not too exhaustive options. One of which was to try again, and I do.

If this was film noir and the hitman was about to shoot my window with his Luger, then the engine would give a splutter and I'd be off like a rocket! In this story it does bugger-all. So I stare at the console, hoping that my staring will effectuate, with the help of some chaos theory butterflies, the engine starting. Now I'm definitely running out of options. I resist looking at the engine because I know that won't achieve anything. Oh, for Pete's sake. I flick the latches on the centre chair and push it back-

Parents never just expect you to call for a chat and children never, ever call their parents just for a chat.

wards. Now I can see the engine. Well, fiddledeedee! I turn the key again as I'm watching the engine and guess what? I may as well have been watching the chair. So now I'm really in a fix. Heuristic processes have abandoned me and I can only think the worst. I'll miss this lunch appointment. The cost to repair this piece of crap will put a big dent in my beer drinking budget. Hair will grow out through my fingernails. The church beckons. At this point I decide, against every message being transmitted to my brain, to phone my father. Even as I pick up the telephone my stomach is shooting flares that spell out:

'DON'T!! BURY THE VAN. SAY YOU LOST IT IN A CARD GAME.'

And still I dial that ever familiar number.

'G'day, son, how can I help you?'

Parents never just expect you to call for a chat and children never, ever call their parents just for a chat.

'Dad, my ah, the Urvan (pause), I turn the key and well, the ... nothing happens.'

'Gee, I'd better get over and have a look at it!'

'I've tried everything, Dad.' In my repertoire anyway.

'Really. Uh-huh. Then I don't know, son.'

At last, after twenty-eight years on this dad-forsaken planet, we are of equal standing. Two men confused and without any idea. This bond lasted possibly one second and then the intangible hierarchy cemented itself forever.

'Say, son, did you check the battery?'

Now I should have deliberated on this question. But one can get drunk on such a powerful bond. Even though I am aware of my lack of common car sense, I am still full of shit. Also I know my vehicle better than anybody. I have had it for two years. I have never seen the battery. So, applying an awkward syllogism and fuelled by the enjoyment of the moment I was sharing with my father, I replied, 'Dad, it's a diesel. It doesn't have a battery.'

By the bye, it does have a battery. It sits behind the driver's seat covered by a metal casing. You know what they say — outa sight, outa mind.

There was a pause. Long enough to let me know that I may have uttered the most stupid statement in the history of communication. Then dad said, 'Check the battery, son.'

At my father's funeral I told that story as part of his eulogy. It explained a verse of a poem I had written for him called 'My Father's Laugh'. Afterwards, many of his old mates came up to shake my hand. Each one looked at me and sotto voce, almost to themselves, said 'The battery, heh, heh.' My father's laugh continues to be such an important vehicle for me. While I keep that in good repair I reckon I can handle the potholes and blind spots as well as 'the slings and arrows'.

Now, on with the carnival.

JON DOUST

ROAD RAGE

Road Rage? It's getting worse. Next person I see with Road Rage I'm going to get out of my car and beat the hell out of them. But I wouldn't. Not me. You see, I've got Road Calm.

Road Calm? Yes. Ten years of hard work have given me serenity in my car. I drive in an altered state. I might be driving the car, but I'm travelling astrally. I have it down to a fine art. As soon as the car is on its way, I'm in meditation mode. If you are on a road while I am you can do anything you like, I'll give way. You can have the parking bay, the left-lane, the right-lane, whatever. Truth is, after many, younger years living like I didn't want to live, now I live like I want to live.

Here's what happens when I'm on the road.

I'm driving down a major freeway and a bloke in the left-lane up ahead cuts into a bloke beside him, on his right. Horns blare and he returns to his lane. As I pull alongside I can see he is about to do it again. I apply the brakes, let him through, smile brightly in his rear-view mirror and wave a jolly, merry Christmas sort of wave. Even at that distance I can see the blood flood his face and the fist rise with it. Road Rage meets Road Calm.

To be straight, before the electro-shock therapy, the birth of my son and my giving up all things hallucinogenic, I was just as tense on the road. You cut me off and both my hands were on the horn, my toes would give you fingers and my head would spin with wild-eyed rage. Nobody said I had anything in particular. There was no off-the-shelf term. People thought I was crazy, sure. People thought I was a bit aggressive on the road, sure. People thought the authorities should take away my licence, sure, and they did, but nobody ever said I had Rage.

Here's what happens to some people when you try to do good. I'm driving towards a round-about. I see a bloke has got there before me and is waiting. I wave him on. He waves me on. I give him the thumbs up. As I drive past he gives me the 'You're a wanker' sign and I see a face full of disdain for someone who made a goodwill gesture. This man has Road Rage for people who have Road Calm. Later, at the end of the day, I allow myself to imagine I have Road Rage. I drive my car at 60km per hour into his front door and I see the look of disdain switch to one of surprise and horror as his door and he become one and the same. When I open my eyes, I feel no rage, but an

This proved very useful because later that night in the lockup I was able to entertain the truly dangerous criminal types by blowing bubbles of blood through that same hole.

even greater sense of calm. I'm ready for a three day drive.

During the storm before the Calm, the people who thought the authorities should take away my licence saw to it that they did. There was the time I ploughed through a bus shelter and snapped a light pole off at the base, helped by a state so drunken I felt no pain when the metal horn broke off and penetrated my upper lip. This proved very useful because later that night in the lockup I was able to entertain the truly dangerous criminal types by blowing bubbles of blood through that same hole. They thought this hilarious and stopped short of thumping me seriously because I wore a suit and looked like a nice, wussy, middle-class boy. Then there was the time my mate said he needed to make a phone call and I parked the car inside the phone box. Difficult manoeuvre, sure, and helped considerably by the slab of beer we consumed down by the old jetty in a futile attempt to prove we were men before our time. The phone, by the way, was out of order and the question still crops up from time to time: 'Was the phone already out of order, or was it out of order as a result of my surrealistic parking?'

Here's what can happen when I make a mistake and you're behind me. I'm driving towards the traffic lights. I forget to put on the right-hand blinker. I stop because the light is red. As I stop, I realise my mistake and flick the lever. There's a person behind me. She sees the right-hand blink. She sees red and green at the same time. She gives me fingers, fists, violent head movements, the lot. I remain calm and notice her violence does not make her ugly. For a second I imagine she is trying to seduce me. She gets out of her car, rips my door off, and launches herself at me in a passionate, uncontrollable explosion of lust. I laugh at my audacity. She screams at my effrontery. All the while I'm counting the seconds before I move away and she can continue in the direction she expected before my surprise blink. It is all of eight. For an eight-second loss of time I have been fingered, condemned and desired dead? Not seduced. Well, not really.

Here's what can happen when I make a big mistake. I'm parked in a quiet suburban street. I move out real slow from the curb and fail to see a bloke coming at me. He hits the horn, the mouth, the arms, legs and the person sitting next to him. The car rocks with his rage. On this day my Road Calm is at full strength. I'm almost asleep. I fail to notice him. I have done wrong. My trance-like speed is so slow a person without Road Rage would think I was stationary, but I go for a soft glide to the left, then a full-stop. As the Road Rager rocks by I crawl out of the car and kneel on the bitumen in prayer position, begging for forgiveness. He drives his car into a Telstra van.

This is what can happen to people who lose it completely. I'm parking my car. I have not yet completed the task. Behind me I see a man in a four-wheel drive who seems very interested in my manoeuvring. His machine is clean, shiny, bought for suburban use only and one of those brutes with the Cruise Missile attachments. I'm careful, calm and working on another position when the man begins jumping up and down in his seat. He springs from the cockpit, yelling, screaming and gesticulating with everything that can be gesticulated, pumping his pump-action shotgun and firing at will. When he reaches my car and sees my Calm the tiny morsel of temper he hasn't yet lost becomes irretrievable and he calls for air support from the Stealth bomber above. His body heat steam-cleans his suit and causes schools in the immediate area to send children home for the day. All because he thinks I might do something I haven't done yet. And I don't do it. But for him it's too late. The Cruise missiles, heat seekers, find their mark. Where once there was a parking bay there's now a hole, gaping.

Here's what I've done. I went and bought myself a Prime earth-mover. One of those monstrous machines you see carting dirt out of open-cut mines. In the back I've built a small house, a jacuzzi, a nice little Japanese garden and an ashram. Last week on Highway 1, I ran into twenty-seven Road Ragers and all are now permanent residents of the ashram. It's quite remarkable. We have no more trouble on the roads. If you see us, it's best to stay clear. Sometimes we're so calm we fall asleep.

JOHN RYAN

THE CHILD PERSON

Dylan could tell Phaedra was just as anxious as him. Where his method of dealing with anxiety was to pick his toe-jam through the lattice of his Bali sandals, then flick it under the seat, hers was to alternately scrunch and unscrunch the tie-dyed sarong she had bought from the Darwin beach market five years ago.

What a trip that had been. In more ways than one. Happy times. A grant from the Arts Council to teach the locals the art of carving Paul Keating figurines from turtle-shell. Perfect; sun, sand, surf. And then some arsehole has to go and show that the turtles were nearly extinct! Well, it was fun while it lasted. Not like today. Summonsed. You did not find yourself sitting in the Ravi Shankar Room waiting for Shogun unless there was a good reason. Which meant Elvis had once

Happy times. A grant from the Arts Council to teach the locals the art of carving Paul Keating figurines from turtle-shell.

again

done something to disgrace them here at the Enclave of Knowledge, Enlightenment and Love.

As if their minds were welded to the same thought, Phaedra turned big concerned eyes on him. They met, then broke away.

Phaedra muttered, 'The bio-rythms indicated a crisis. I warned you.'

Which was true. He'd hoped this time she'd be wrong. Last time she'd consulted the bio-rythms they'd predicted sexual abstinence for a year. 326 days later, they were looking pretty accurate. But better not to think of THAT.

Dylan tuned in to the background music. The Mahavishnu Orchestra segued into Yothu Yindi. One thing about Shogun, he had a fabulous sound system.

The sound of a door opening snapped him to. Shogun strode into the room in his black leather boots and kimono, climbed the steps to his small raised platform and sat cross-legged.

Looking straight at them, he spoke in that

booming voice, most feared and all respected.

'It's about your child-person, Elvis.'

From the corner of his eye, Dylan saw Phaedra bite her bottom lip. Shogun continued.

'Ever since he came to us here at the Enclave of Knowledge, Enlightenment and Love, he's been a real pain in the arse. But today things really came to a head. The rock of his spirituality has been totally eaten away by the eternal dripping of earthly delights.'

'What exactly do you mean?' asked Phaedra.

'He's fucked. He's been doing well in the less important subjects like reading and spelling, but it's his attitude. Last week he put superphosphate in his nature plot ...'

Dylan could feel Phaedra wince as if a knife had been shoved into her spleen.

'... and he's been putting horse manure on the vegetables.'

Some vestige of fatherly protection rose in Dylan and made him speak. 'Well, that's okay, isn't it?'

Shogun glared. 'After they're cooked? But the straw that broke the Dalai Lama's back came in Biol. I found him hunched over his Bunsen burner barbecuing this.'

So saying, Shogun tossed something at Dylan. The fetid cube landed in Dylan's lap. Gingerly his fingers moved out to touch. They recoiled immediately at the rubbery texture.

'What is it?'

'Steak.'

Phaedra could contain the tears no longer.

Shogun stood. 'He was offering it to the other child-people. Fortunately I convinced them it was hash.'

Through her tears, Phaedra spoke haltingly. 'Last week, as I was putting his dirty clothes back in his basket, I found a polony sandwich hidden under his pot. I tried to talk but we just can't rap.'

Again Dylan felt impelled to offer a better picture of his son. 'He was such a gentle baby-person, gurgling his mantras in his saffron nappy.' As he spoke, the thought occurred to Dylan, 'What if it hadn't been saffron after all?' But he kept this to himself and ploughed on. 'I'd read to him from *Hitch Hiker's Guide to the Galaxy* and his dear old Grandma would tell him fairy stories about the good ol' days before Fraser turned out the lights.'

Shogun said, 'We often find problems start in the home. You don't mind if I ask you some personal questions?'

What could they do but shake their heads?

'You are married?'

'Yes,' said Dylan.

Shogun let out a low disapproving groan.

'Our parents threatened to cut off our pocket-money if we didn't, ' explained Phaedra.

'We find that threats and punishment never

work. Why, only last week I sent a memo to all the staff saying that any teacher found reprimanding a child-person, would be instantly dismissed without severance pay.'

Phaedra threw out her hands. 'But what can you do when he starts playing Snap with your tarot cards?'

True, thought Dylan, remembering his own efforts, slaving away all day making Elvis a beautiful kelp soufflé with a swede and parsnip side salad, only to later find it untouched, while a telltale Whopper wrapper was jammed down in the bottom of his satchel.

Shogun mused. 'Maybe he's not getting enough love?'

Dylan snapped. 'Love? His grandmother missed four aerobics classes to knit him a macramé football. Do you think he was grateful? All he did was kick it around the house.'

Phaedra rejoined, 'I even took him down to the dole office to fill in his first form and he dobbed me in.'

Shogun's eyebrows rose. 'What happened to your leather shop?'

Phaedra explained how their new belief-system prevented them from touching the skin of dead animals.

As she talked, Dylan remembered with sadness the frustration of trying to make sandals out of Lebanese bread. While they looked good, they just didn't wear very well. He was still too humiliated to share the experience with Shogun.

God, how he regretted taking on their new belief-system. But Phaedra had been adamant. 'We'll cover any losses with our fresh juice stall at the markets,' she'd said. Then Mr Juicy cut off their supply of concentrate and they were stuffed.

Shogun had listened patiently to Phaedra. 'Have you thought of a psychiatrist for Elvis?'

'No. But we've had the vet around.'

'Vet?'

'Yes, Elvis was a horse in his former life.'

Shogun took a deep breath. 'Well, I'm sorry but I can't see any place

Shogun's face bespoke alarm. 'Dib dib dib, dob dob dob? I paid three hundred bucks for that mantra.'

for him here. His telepathy teacher tells me Elvis refuses to take mental notes, he wears sunglasses to Iridology and Speedos to the nude swimming classes. And anyway, this morning he ran away.'

Both parents blurted, 'What?'

Shogun handed across a piece of paper. 'He sent me this e-mail about an hour ago.'

Phaedra grabbed it and passed it quickly to Dylan. It read, 'Have run away to join Scouts. Elvis.'

Shogun was mystified. 'These Scouts are obviously some cult or other?'

Dylan knew he'd heard the word before. He was searching through mists to find it. Ever since the Rebirth and Colonic Irrigation, the past had been nothing but a miso soup.

Phaedra put in, 'I've heard him in his room going Dib dib dib, dob dob dob.'

Shogun's face bespoke alarm. 'Dib dib dib, dob dob dob? I paid three hundred bucks for that mantra.'

Quickly he vaulted down from the platform and moved to a computer keyboard. 'Let's see what it's got on the Net.'

Shogun hammered in commands. 'It says here they camp in the bush.'

'Communing with nature, that's okay,' enthused Phaedra.

Shogun continued to read, 'And they have a motto, "Be prepared!" '

Dylan's heart jumped. That was what he'd always said himself. He didn't have three hundred kilos of freeze-dried Nasi Goreng in the fallout shelter for nothing.

Phaedra was more animated than any time since she'd mistakenly put sugar in the cookies instead of dope. 'It all makes sense. The other day he came home and said he needed a woggle. I told him to go to his room and do it in private but then he told me he needed a gumnut with a hole in it.'

Dylan couldn't help himself. 'Poor kid must be desperate.'

Shogun spun round the computer screen. 'Look at these hats they wear. They must have funny shaped heads?'

Dylan said nothing at this ignorance. Obviously, they used the hats to squeeze the juice out of some giant bush oranges.

Shogun read on. 'It says something about their initiation being run by a woman called Akela.'

'An earth mother. Groovy.' Phaedra's tears had given way to smiles.

Instinctively Dylan turned to meet Phaedra's kiss. It found his lips, flush. They clasped hands, rose as one, and walked towards the door.

'I haven't dismissed you yet,' wailed Shogun, striking his boots with a leather crop.

'No, but we've dismissed you,' said Dylan, and felt Phaedra's hand squeeze into his, the way it used to when Tama Shud had struck the first chord of a Love-In.

'Elvis has shown us the way,' added Phaedra. 'Now, we too must join these Scouts.'

They left the room, Dylan walking on air. The miso was still too thick for specifics, but he knew that this was the right path. Already he was vaguely recalling more about 'scouts' — men wearing woollen skirts and eating stuffed sheep's stomach on New Year's Eve, the wheezy sound of some musical instrument and something about making fires by rubbing sticks. And constant masturbation. Not that there would be any need of that. Not with the way Phaedra was rubbing his inside thigh. The bio-rythms weren't going to be right after all.

Outside, Dylan sniffed the petrol fumes and his heart burst with joy. In a way, he was already touching the skins of long-dead animals. After a night of incense, flavoured tofu and rumpy-pumpy, Phaedra would come round. They could start up the leather shop again, sing all the old Quintessence numbers, laugh. And they would have Elvis to thank for it all. Elvis really was a chip off the old chapatti.

Things were looking up.

CONTRIBUTORS NOTES

Dennis Altman, born in 1943, is one of Australia's leading political and social commentators. He studied at Cornell University in the 1960s and has lectured in politics at Monash, Sydney and La Trobe universities. His first book, *Homosexual*, was published in 1991 and there have been many since, including one on the politics of stamps, his first novel — *The Comfort of Men*, the work *Power and Community: Organisational and Cultural Responses to AIDS*, and in 1997 his autobiography, *Defying Gravity: a Political Life*.

Steve Bedwell is, at various times, a writer, producer and performer on both television and radio. He is also a stand-up comedian and author. During his time as writer of questions for the ABC Children's TV game show 'Vidiot', Steve was highlighted on 'Backchat' for his question: John Farnham had a hit in the 1960s with the song, 'Sadie The ...': a) Washing Lady; b) Ironing Lady; c) Cleaning Lady; d) Unmarried Mother.

Currently domiciled in Melbourne, Steve appears on Melbourne radio MMM.

Bruce Beresford was born and educated in Sydney. A film and opera director, his films include *Don's Party*, *Breaker Morant*, *Tender Mercies*, *Black Robe*, *Driving Miss Daisy* and *Paradise Road*; his operas include *Girl of the Wild West* (Spoleto Festival, Italy), *Elektra* (South Australian Opera) and *Sweeney Todd* (Portland Opera, Unites States).

Libby-Jane Charleston was born in 1968, grew up in Perth and began writing in her teens. She completed a BA in English at Curtin University and has been working as a radio journalist, newspaper columnist and television reporter. She has lived in Hong Kong where she was a well-known television news reader and won the *South China Morning Post* short story award. Her poems appear in the 1997 anthology of the International Society of Poets. She lives in Sydney with her husband Paul, where she continues to work as a journalist and is writing her first novel.

Barry Cohen was a Federal Member of Parliament from 1969 to 1990, and Minister for Arts, Heritage and Environment from 1983 to 1987. He has published four books — *Life of the Party*, *After the Party*, *How to Become Prime Minister* and *Life with Gough*. A new book, *From Whitlam to Winston,* is due out in late 1997. He has also been a columnist at various times for the *Bulletin*, the *Australian*, the Melbourne *Herald-Sun* and *Time*.

He is married with three sons, and lives on the central coast of New South Wales at Gosford.

The Coodabeen Champions have been broadcasting since 1981. In that time the troupe have never missed a Saturday morning, 10am–Midday, first on 3RRR, then 3LO, and since 1993, 3AW.

Between 1988 and 1996 the Coodabeens broadcast to the whole of Australia and beyond with their weekly Sunday night program on ABC Radio, which covered everything under the sun. Part of both the Saturday Footy show, and Sunday nights, has been a 'trademark' talkback segment where 'listeners' phone Tony Leonard with queries and stories.

Don from Devonport has been a regular caller, who always puts a Tasmanian spin on things. The call from Donny in this volume was broadcast live and later collected onto the ABC CD *Classic Cricket Hits*. The CD also contains troupe member Greg Champion's 'I Made a Hundred in the Backyard at Mum's'.

Santo Cilauro started working in student reviews in the mid-80s. With his collaborators from that time, Tom Gleisner and Rob Stich, he has joined up with Jane Kennedy and gone on to popular success and critical acclaim in both radio and television with such shows as 'Frontline', 'The Late Show' and 'Funky Squad'. More recently the Frontline team have turned their attention to feature films with *The Castle*.

Max Cullen, well known as an actor, began as a copy-boy in 1956 on the *Sydney Morning Herald*. He subsequently worked for almost every newspaper and magazine publisher in Sydney as lay-out artist, illustrator and cartoonist. He attended Julian Ashton's Art School and also studied sculpture under Lyndon Dadswell. He continues to do illustration for books and magazines as well as exhibiting his paintings and sculpture. Since 1990 he has worked on the Channel Nine 'Sunday' Program as arts reporter. He is a published poet and short story writer and is constantly writing the novel.

David Dale graduated in psychology from Sydney University but decided he would do less harm to the cause of mental health if he moved into journalism. He's been a political reporter for the *Australian*, Editor of the *Bulletin*, and breakfast broadcaster for ABC radio, and he currently edits a daily column called 'Stay in Touch' for the *Sydney Morning Herald*. His eight books include *The 100 Things Everyone Needs To Know About Australia* and *Essential Places — a book about ideas and where they started.*

Paul Dempsey grew up in Wagga Wagga. He emblazoned numerous jobs in his homeland with his colourful personality before finding himself at the cutting edge of Australian–Vietnam trade in the late 1980s. Still resident in Vietnam, he is now country chief of an international firm.

Barry Dickins is the unapologetic grandson of a murderer, court reporter, archangel and Supreme Court magistrate. His current occupation is journalist. Dickins is author of the stage play *Remember Ronald Ryan*, a look at the life of Ronald Joseph Ryan, the last person hanged in Australia, which was presented by Playbox Theatre in Melbourne and won the Victorian Premiers Award for Drama in 1995.

Jon Doust was born in the small Western Australian town, Bridgetown. He grew up in a family that encouraged kids to make their own fun, and leg-pulling and story-telling were on the top of the list. He went on to work in a bank, a supermarket, shearing sheds, apple orchards, and even managed to gain a BA in English and work for ten years as a journalist. This proved too much for him and he gave it all up for a stable career in comedy. He never recovered.

Tim Gooding is a musician, songwriter and screen-writer. First coming to public notice in the late seventies with the band XL Capris, Gooding has written a novel and a children's book and has a feature film in development *The Tony Sorrento Story*.

Dorinda C Haffner was born in Ghana. A human dynamo, she travels and works nationally and interna-tionally as an artist, public speaker and television presenter, spreading her brand of madness, goodwill and cultural understanding to children, adults and organisations alike.

Claire Haywood is a writer/director originally from Perth. She has worked for The Winter Theatre in Fremantle, Underground Theatre Productions, the Sydney Theatre Company and numerous fringe companies as a freelance director. Her plays include *Christmas Day, It Couldn't Happen to Me* and *Table for One.* She was the recipient of a Literature Board Fellowship in 1995. She currently resides in Sydney with her husband

and three children, and has just completed a short film, *Insomnia*, which she wrote and directed.

Mark 'Jacko' Jackson is a Australian legend. A former top AFL footballer, Jacko had chart success in the early eighties with his song 'I'm an Individual'. This led him on a path to entertainment success that saw him become a Hollywood TV star, and advertising icon as the 'Energiser guy.' These days Jacko lives in Sydney and among many business ventures, owns a gold mine located in the Canadian Yukon.

Linda Jaivin is the author of *Eat Me* and *Rock 'n' Roll Babes from Outer Space*. She is co-editor with Geremie Barmé of *New Ghosts, Old Dreams: Chinese Rebel Voices*. She lives in Sydney.

Catherine Jennings grew up in Western Australia and has been a regular comedy writer and performer, both live and on radio. She is currently living in Geraldton.

Rick Kane has a round but impish face. He has been a student, service station attendant, factory hand, actor, unemployed, teacher, youth education officer and unemployed again. Then an actor, stand-up comic, poet, writer, unemployed, charity door-knocker, encyclopedia salesman, training and development officer, and employment consultant. Currently he is a student at La Trobe. During all this he has grown four inches.

Jacqui Lang is a Perth-born journalist who worked in Western Australia for the *Daily News*, *Weekend News*, Channel Nine and Channel Seven before moving to Sydney in 1990. There she began working as a researcher, reporter and chief of staff for the Hinch current affairs program on Channel Seven, then chief of staff of 'Alan Jones' Live on Network Ten.

In 1994 she began working as a columnist for the showbiz magazine *New Weekly*, where she was later promoted to senior writer. Currently, she is working as a freelance writer from her Paddington home. Her hobbies are reading, going to the movies, eating out, and gossiping.

Hugh Lunn was born in wartime Brisbane and began his newspaper career on the *Courier-Mail* in 1960 before heading for Fleet Street via China and Russia. He worked on the London *Daily Mirror* and was a Reuters correspondent in Vietnam, Singapore and Indonesia. He has won five national awards for feature writing, including three Walkley Awards. His first memoir, *Vietnam: A Reporters War,* was an *Age* Book of the Year, and his next memoir, *Over the Top with Jim,* was the years biggest selling Australian non-fiction book. The popular *Head over Heels* — sequel to *Over the Top with Jim* — followed.

Greg Macainsh was born in Melbourne in 1950. He attended Norwood High School and after failing to get conscripted spent three years at Swinburne Film and Television School. A keen musician and songwriter, he formed the group Skyhooks in 1973. Their debut album 'Living in the Seventies' was the biggest selling record by an Australian group at the time. 'Horror Movie', 'Ego is Not a Dirty Word', 'All My Friends are Getting Married', 'Balwyn Calling' and 'Women in Uniform' are a few of Macainsh's songs that have become Australian music icons. Skyhooks disbanded in 1980 and Macainsh moved into music production and management. A highly successful Skyhooks reformation in 1990 yielded another Macainsh penned tune 'Jukebox in Siberia' which became an Australian number one hit. Macainsh has returned from a lengthy sojourn in Europe and the US and is currently writing and residing in Melbourne.

Shane Maloney is a novelist and columnist; the author of comic crime thrillers *Stiff* and *The Brush-Off.* He has been, at various times, the Director of the Melbourne Comedy Festival (retired), the Public Relations Officer of the Australian Boy Scout's Association (escaped), a contestant on 'Sale of the Century' and 'Jeopardy' (stumped) and a swimming pool lifeguard (sacked). He is currently the Deputy Director of the Brunswick Institute, a weatherboard think tank financed by his wife (much obliged).

Strephyn Mappin is a freelance writer currently residing in Melbourne. He has had two collections of short stories, *Chiaroscuro* and *Heart Murmurs*, published with Fremantle Arts Centre Press. His work has also appeared in several anthologies and won a number of literary awards. Several of his novels for teenagers are currently under development by film companies.

Lex Marinos is Wagga Wagga's most famous son ... well, after Michael Slater, Mark Taylor, Paul Kelly and several hundred other sports people. In fact, in another body Lex could have also been sporting hero. Lex is well-known as a director of live theatre and feature film, a television actor and a sports writer and broadcaster — and what he doesn't know about fishing could be engraved on a trout fly.

Trevor Marmalade, North Melbourne footy fan, is best known for his regular appearances on television with 'The Footy Show' and 'Hey, Hey, It's Saturday'. Trevor has had an extensive career as a live comic and humourous sports broadcaster, and he looks forward to the day when he will back the card at Flemington. Or Caulfield. Or the Moe trots ... or, heck, even get a winner at one of the Wentworth Park dog meets.

Stephen Muecke is the author and editor of a number of books on Australian culture, the most recent being *No Road (bitumen all the way)*. He is Professor of Cultural Studies at the University of Technology, Sydney, and lives in Newtown.

H G Nelson is a Barossa Valley born and bred footballer who has been able to combine the three great loves of all fit Australians, ie Butchering, Banking and Bagging Bloody Great Fish.

His steady climb from abattoir drop box to back door access to the homes of this nation's movers and shakers has been one that has thrilled Asia more than anything since Jean Shrimpton blew in for the Melbourne Cup.

Damien O'Doherty is a Perth-born actor and comedian who is currently residing in Canberra with her personal trainer and their two-year-old daughter.

John Ryan is a writer, comedian and musician, best known as the wild guitarist 'Johnny Leopard'. After disappearing for several years overseas, John has returned to his native Perth where his ambition is to learn a new trade as a croupier, partner Gary Carvolth in a TV talk show and be an AFL boundary umpire.

Rob Sitch began working in student revues in the mid-80s. Stich and his collaborators from that time, Tom Gleisner and Santo Cilauro, joined up with Jane Kennedy and have gone on to achieve popular success and critical acclaim in both radio and television with such shows as 'Frontline', 'The Late Show' and 'Funky Squad'. More recently the Frontline team have turned their attention to feature films with *The Castle.*

Roy Slaven is co-host of 'Club Buggery' on ABC-TV. While Roy has represented Australia in cricket, Rugby League, tennis, athletics, boxing, Greco-Roman wrestling, table tennis, shooting, basketball and swimming, he is perhaps best remembered as trainer/owner of the giant stallion Rooting King, winner of the WS Cox plate, the Villiers, the Sydney Cup and the Melbourne Cup on more occasions than any other horse in the history of Australian racing. Rooting King is thought to have been part of the bloodline that stretches back through Peter Pan and Phar Lap, to Carbine.

Tim Smith is married with two children, a dog, a mortgage, a Charger and hasn't got enough time to be sitting around writing the story of his life ... it would take a lifetime. After numerous successes in live revue and television, Tim is currently to be found sending funniness scampering across MMM airwaves every weekday morning.

Clinton Walker, as the author of such relatively serious tomes as *Stranded*, the forthcoming *Football Life* and the classic Bon Scott biography *Highway to Hell*, rarely enjoys the opportunity to write funny. Contributing to such anthologies as *Men-Love-Sex*, however, was good practice; contributing to John Marsden's *This I Believe* was just funny-peculiar. The piece included here was originally published in *The Edge*; only the proper nouns have been changed, etc etc ... Walker is currently working on a book about Aboriginal performers in Australian popular music.

Dave Warner, author of the novels *City Of Light* and *Big Bad Blood*, is also a musician, screen-writer and broadcaster. Having growing up in Perth, Dave now lives in Sydney with wife Nicole and baby Violet.

Wilbur Wilde is best known as a member of the 'Hey, Hey, It's Saturday' team. Wilbur has been a part of the television show for thirteen of its twenty-five years and looks forward to the next millennium as 'Hey Hey' goes from strength to strength. He still loves music and writes fiction now and then.